SAM IN THE CLOUDS

BY:
CAMERON DE JONG

Published by Cameron De Jong

This book is dedicated to Sam, CJ, Wolf, Oliver, Cori, Duke, Redick, Kacy, Winston, and Dexter. I know you are all looking down from doggy heaven.

Very special **THANK YOU** to **Annette** and **Yvette** for their feedback and friendship.

Stay in touch at https://samintheclouds.com

ISBN 979-8-89965-474-9 (Paperback)

ISBN 979-8-89965-471-8 (ePub)

CONTENTS

INTRODUCTION

Sam in the Clouds emerged from the cherished terrain of childhood memory—a story inspired by the profound connection my sister Jaime and I shared with our first and most beloved dog, Sam.

From my earliest memories, Sam was simply there, a steadfast, brown-and-white heart beating at the center of our family. But Sam was never *just a pet*. He was our four-legged guardian spirit, the furry keeper of our whispered secrets, the tireless playmate in our sprawling four-acre yard, and the silent, joyful shadow tailing us as we chased fireflies into the deepening summer twilight, only turning for home when the last light faded.

His personality quirks remain vivid in our memories despite the years: his unexpected love for lollipops (he would hold the stick while enjoying the sweet treat, which never failed to make us laugh), and his legendary fear of thunderstorms that once sent him bolting four houses down our street, crashing through a neighbor's door seeking refuge. Though the bathtub was typically his sanctuary during storms, that particular night nothing would do but finding human comfort, wherever it might be. Sam embodied wonderful contradictions—fiercely protective of his family yet comically terrified of nature's light shows. But it was these very idiosyncrasies that made him uniquely ours, that singular blend of courage and vulnerability that taught us the true depth of love.

He was my father's best friend first and foremost—their bond was special and immediate—but Sam became a best friend to our entire family, adapting to exactly what each of us needed from him. Though he spent most of his time indoors with us, his occasional ventures into the backyard were always moments of joy, as if every blade of grass deserved his careful inspection.

When cancer took Sam while Jaime and I were still young, we felt his loss acutely. That profound experience of childhood grief became the seed from which this novel grew, though the story itself takes a fictional journey far beyond our actual experiences.

This novel is fiction loosely inspired by real elements of our lives with Sam. Through William's journey, I've created a tapestry that explores how loss can open doorways to a more profound understanding, how family bonds strengthen when tested by grief's heavy hand, and how connections between worlds might be more accessible than we typically believe.

Sam in the Clouds isn't just about a boy and his departed dog but about the simple faith that sustains us through difficult times—the belief that love, once given, never truly ends but transforms into something that remains with us always. It's about finding meaning in loss and recognizing that what appears to be an ending might just be a new beginning in an unexpected form.

I hope that readers will find in William's story echoes of their own experiences with beloved companions who have crossed beyond ordinary sight yet somehow remain present in our hearts. Perhaps they'll consider, as I have while writing this story, that the boundaries we assume to be absolute might actually be more permeable than we imagine.

Chapter 1:
The Shape in the Sky

Silence woke me at 3:17 a.m.—the void where Sam's paws should have clicked against hardwood. My hand reached automatically to the empty space beside my bed, finding only cold air instead of warm fur. For the first time in thirteen years, I faced the darkness alone, without the steady rhythm of Sam's breathing to anchor the night. Only the merciless ticking of my clock remained, counting seconds into a new, unbearable reality.

Three days since we'd buried him, and already the world felt wrong, tilted off its axis—as if gravity itself had been recalibrated in his absence. I'd been prepared for sadness when the veterinarian first mentioned cancer. What I hadn't expected was this suffocating alteration of everything I knew: the morning light seemed to leach its color before my eyes, leaving only thin, grey washes against my window; the very air in the house felt scoured, each breath a conscious effort in its unnerving thinness; ordinary sounds—a closing door, Mom's distant piano—now cracked through the silence, sharp and startling, echoing in the new, yawning spaces he'd left behind. How could the disappearance of one medium-sized dog create such a vast, echoing emptiness?

I didn't cry. Not anymore. The well of tears had run dry sometime during that first endless night. What remained was something harder to name—a cold, hollow space that seemed to have taken up residence in my chest, pulsing with a dull ache at each heartbeat, a question without an answer.

Then a thin, unusual glow seeped beneath my curtains—not the fleeting slash of headlights nor the gentle advance of dawn. An odd quality to the light pulled me from bed, drawing me to the window that overlooked the backyard oak, its roots now gripping the freshly turned earth of Sam's grave.

My eyes caught on his bed. The blue blanket still held a barely discernible, heart-aching impression—the ghost of the weight that used to comfort me there. My own breath hitched, and I had to physically press a hand to my chest, as if to contain the way the hollow ache gnawed its way further inside me where his warmth used to be. How many nights had I drifted off to the sound of his gentle, rhythmic sighs from that spot, a comforting presence in the hushed stillness of the dark? He'd even nudged his way there, a trembling but determined guardian, during that terrifying Fourth of July when fireworks seemed to shake the whole house. Had I missed something? Some sign he wasn't well? The thought, unwelcome, flickered before I pushed it away.

Three days had passed since Dad's shovel bit into the earth beneath the big oak. Three days since Mom wrapped him in his favorite plaid blanket, the worn tennis ball tucked beside him.

Three days of navigating a house suddenly unfamiliar, tilted off its axis.

I rolled away from the empty bed, the ghost image of that faint impression already searing itself behind my eyelids. Under my desk, the green fuzz of another tennis ball peeked out, its surface deeply scored with teeth marks. My breath hitched; a sudden, sharp pang shot through me—this was the twin to the one Mom had tucked beside him in the grave. My foot nudged it, a small, involuntary twitch that sent the ball thudding against the wall. The sound echoed through the room, stark and incomplete—a question unanswered by Sam's familiar, scrambling paws.

The echo of him, of Sam, lingered everywhere: in the barely visible scratches clawed beside the door during that terrifying Fourth of July bombardment... the time he'd comically tried to "herd" the runaway lawnmower. The frayed comforter edge he'd tug when I overslept. Photos pinned above my desk mocked me with happier times: Sam as a clumsy puppy, his eyes already holding a disarming wisdom; Sam, stick held delicately in his teeth, eyes half-closed in bliss as he savored a stolen cherry lollipop Lyn had left on the counter; Sam dripping, joyful, at the creek; Sam on the porch, listening to my guitar practice with a patient focus no human ever managed.

He transcended ordinary canine existence. "An old soul," Mrs. Peterson called him. He would incline his head thoughtfully, those knowing, soulful brown eyes absorbing the world's complexities, perceiving dimensions beyond mere physical reality. I remembered the afternoon before eighth grade began—my stomach a cold knot of anxiety, certain Tyler Westfield would make the year a fresh misery—Sam had rested his head deliberately on my knee. His gaze met mine, and a current of understanding flowed between us—not mere animal comfort, but a profound reassurance that settled my racing thoughts and affirmed some hidden resilience within me. He possessed an uncanny awareness. He would materialize, a stabilizing force, whenever Mom suffered migraines—I recalled finding her once, complexion ashen, features tight with pain, Sam resting his head on her lap until the episode subsided—or when Lyn encountered teenage turmoil, often easing her door ajar and waiting patiently, a silent invitation for emotional unburdening. A protector in weathered fur.

Last year, when Dad's construction company nearly went under and the arguments about money echoed through these walls nightly, Sam had somehow known exactly what to do. One especially bad night—Dad's voice rising about loans, Mom's desperate counter about keeping the house—I'd found Sam methodically gathering his toys from around the house, depositing them in the living room between my arguing parents. The pile grew: tennis ball, rope toy, squeaky carrot, rubber bone. They'd stopped mid-sentence, confusion breaking the tension.

Then Lyn had giggled, pointing at Sam sitting proudly beside his offering. "He's giving you all his stuff to sell." The sheer absurdity of it cracked the tension—Dad let out a sudden bark of laughter, Mom's hand flew to her mouth, and the tears brimming in her eyes shifted from despair to a startled, washing relief. Something had shifted that night.

Dad found the Millfield contract the next week. Sam had bridged the unbridgeable, not with words but with a dog's pure, problem-solving love. Now, facing breakfast without him, the chasm between us all yawned so wide, so deep, that no bridge seemed to span it.

The kitchen air, usually comforting with the scent of coffee, now felt tight, overlaid with the almost frantic sweetness of cinnamon from Mom's pre-dawn baking. Her movements were too quick, almost jerky, as she flipped French toast, her shoulders hunched as if bracing against a chill only she felt. The thin gold chain of her usual cross lay against her collarbone, a glint of constancy.

"Morning, Will." She offered a smile that didn't quite reach her eyes, a brittle curve of her lips. "Hungry?"

French toast. My favorite—a dish usually reserved for birthdays, for celebration. A wave of nausea tightened my throat at the sight of it now; the intended kindness felt like a cruel mockery of all that was festive and good.

"A little," I lied, the word catching in my throat as I slid into my chair. My stomach clenched, heavy and unresponsive as a bag of stones.

Dad sat opposite, the newspaper a fortress wall between us. His work clothes, usually fitting his solid frame, now hung a little loose. Shadows, like old bruises, pooled beneath his eyes; a dark stubble crept across his jaw. The paper rustled, then lowered just enough for his eyes—red-rimmed and weary—to find mine over the top edge. His jaw looked tight, as if he were bracing himself. A brief nod.

"Sleep okay?" His voice rasped, the sound gravelly and unfamiliar.

"Yeah."

The lie hung thin in the air between us. He offered a noncommittal grunt before the paper barrier rose once more, shielding him behind sports scores. The world outside kept clicking along, oblivious to ours.

Mom set the plate before me—two golden slices of French toast, the powdered sugar sifted with her usual care. Her hand brushed my shoulder, lingering a breath too long.

That small, deliberate tenderness pierced me more sharply than Dad's coiled stillness.

"Thanks," I managed.

"Will!" Lyn's voice, already edged with pre-teen impatience, cracked through the room. "Used all the hot water again?"

She stood in the doorway, towel-turbaned hair dripping onto the shoulders of her soccer jersey, one hand on her hip, her free foot tapping an irritable rhythm against the doorframe. Twelve years old and usually owning every space she entered, though today her confidence seemed brittle.

"Didn't shower," I muttered into my plate.

Her hand dropped from her hip, and the foot-tapping ceased. The irritation on her face wavered, a flush of embarrassment creeping up her neck. "Oh. Well... someone did."

She slumped into her chair, pointedly avoiding my eyes.

"Probably your mother," Dad said, the newspaper crackling as he folded it with sharp precision. "Up before dawn." An observation heavy with unspoken worry.

"Couldn't sleep," Mom said, bringing her own plate. "Thought I'd be productive."

"Need rest, Marie," Dad countered, his tone softening almost imperceptibly. "Can't fix this by running yourself ragged."

A flicker of something—weariness, perhaps a flash of her own tightly leashed frustration—crossed Mom's face before her lips thinned. "I know, Albert," she said, her voice barely a whisper. "It's just..." Her gaze snagged on Sam's leash, still hanging by the back door, a tangible reminder of all the sounds now missing. "The quiet gets loud."

The word quiet settled over the room, a heavy, suffocating blanket where Sam's once-constant, life-affirming sounds— the happy jingle of his collar, the click of his paws on hardwood—should have been. His absence felt like a physical presence filling the void.

"Can I skip morning classes?" Lyn asked, pushing her toast around. "Maddy's mom—"

"You're going," Dad cut her off flatly. "Full day."

"But—"

"No." His palm hit the table—not a slam, but enough to make forks jump. "Life doesn't stop." He swallowed hard. "Doesn't stop."

"Fine." Lyn stabbed her toast. "Whatever."

"I know it's hard," Mom began, her hand reaching towards Lyn's arm.

"Don't!" Lyn recoiled as if Mom's touch were a live coal, her chair scraping back harshly.

Her face, which had been pale with embarrassment moments before, now flushed a painful red, and the unshed tears that had welled in her eyes seemed to sharpen into angry sparks.

"You don't know!" she cried, her voice thin and cracking. "You're all just acting like it's okay, like... like he didn't matter!" She shoved back further from the table, the legs of her chair screaming against the floor.

"I'm not hungry." Snatching her backpack from the floor, she bolted, the screen door slamming behind her with a shuddering bang that seemed to vibrate through the already taut silence of the kitchen. I flinched, hunching my shoulders as if expecting another blow, the familiar weight of their unspoken miseries pressing down on me.

Mom sighed, pressing her temples. That old, known ache twisted in my chest. It wasn't just Sam's barks or the click of his paws that were missing; it was his subtle alchemy. I remembered one Saturday morning, not unlike this—Dad

12

stressed about a job, Mom worried about bills, Lyn and I bickering—the tension thick enough to curdle milk. Then

Sam, with that uncanny sense of his, had trotted in, nudged Dad's hand until he absently stroked an ear, then settled with a contented sigh at Mom's feet, somehow drawing us all briefly back to the simple, steady calm he radiated just by being there. The argument had just... dissolved. Now, the hollow silence only amplified the chasms between us.

"She'll manage," Dad said after a moment. "Just needs..." He didn't finish.

"We all do," Mom murmured, meeting his eyes. That silent conversation again, years of shared life passing between them.

Dad grunted, drained his coffee, and pushed his chair back. "The Millfield site won't run

itself." He squeezed Mom's shoulder. "Call me."

"We'll be fine."

He stopped beside me. Hesitated. An awkward pat landed on my shoulder. "Hang in," he mumbled, gruffness thick with unshed emotion. Then he was gone, the quiet click of the door amplifying the silence.

Mom and I sat. Just the clock ticking. I swirled syrup.

"Don't have to eat it," Mom said finally. "Cereal?"

I shook my head. "Not hungry." Her worry was a palpable thing. "I'll get lunch at school. Promise," I said, meaning it despite my lack of appetite.

She began clearing plates, efficient and automatic. "Bus in twenty."

Acknowledging her with a slight dip of my chin, I pushed

back from the table. My eyes caught on Sam's water bowl. Still half-full. Untouched. A relic from a world that ended three days ago.

Mom followed my eyes, her hands pausing mid-motion. "Keep meaning to put it away," she whispered.

"Haven't been able to." "Don't," I heard myself say.

"Please." Her head moved in a slow, almost imperceptible affirmation, a flicker of shared understanding warming her tired eyes.

"When we're ready."

The morning routine felt muffled, distant. Brushing teeth, dragging a comb through hair, shoving books—were they even the right ones?—into my bag. Mom retreated to the living room; melancholy piano notes drifted down the hall, tightening my throat.

I slipped out the front door. Cool April air, damp earth smell, sky heavy with unfallen rain. Lyn waited at the end of the drive with Madison, heads together. I stayed back on the porch. My attention fixed on the oak, its branches just beginning to fuzz green.

Beneath it, the disturbed earth. Sam's grave. The word felt foreign, wrong against my tongue. The memory surfaced—the three of us huddled around that raw, open wound in the earth, Sam wrapped in his plaid blanket, looking only asleep. Mom's voice, cracking on the final scripture.

Dad's hand, a vise on my shoulder. Lyn's angry, helpless tears as she clutched his worn collar. And me... I remember the thud of the first clods of dirt hitting the blanket, each one building the wall of numb disbelief higher between me and the world.

Sam in the Clouds

"Bus!" Lyn yelled, jolting me. "Will!"

I stepped off the porch, my feet dragging toward the road. As I neared them, that prickling awareness crawled up my neck. *Being watched.* I scanned the house and the fields. Empty. Still.

My view lifted instinctively. Clouds shifted, parted by sudden wind currents, their undersides tinged with morning color. And then—clearer than thought, more vivid than memory— I saw it. High up, nestled in the curve of one vast, billowing cloud. Not random shapes. A deliberate form. A dog's head, tilted with familiar curiosity. The clouds defined a floppy ear—his ear. Sculpted the gentle, unmistakable uplift of a smile. Sam's smile.

Wise. Patient. Looking down.

My heart seized, then began to hammer so violently I felt its frantic pulse beat up into my throat. My breath snagged somewhere between my lungs and the sky. No. Clouds don't hold form; don't smile. My mind screamed it. Yet the image held—it was him.

Impossibly, undeniably, wonderfully real. I blinked, a desperate spasm, trying to either shatter the illusion or sear it into my memory. A breath of wind answered, teasing the edges of the cloud. The smile blurred, its lines wavered, and then it dissolved back into shapeless vapor. Gone. But the warmth of that connection lingered, a peaceful, freeing current against the persistent chill inside me.

"Will! THE BUS IS LEAVING!" Lyn shouted impatiently from the vehicle steps. The pneumatic doors wheezed open.

Reluctantly, I tore my vision from the sky. On the bus, the mundane world of worn seats and chattering classmates did little to dispel the image. Psychological projection, my brain supplied, a textbook term. Pareidolia—just pattern-seeking neurons doing what they do. My mind clung to these rational anchors, desperate to tether itself to the known. Wishful thinking, that's all. Grief twisting clouds into comfort.

But the explanations felt flimsy, unraveling against the sheer, undeniable force of that memory: the distinct tilt of his head, the gentle uplift of that smile. It wasn't just any dog shape. It was Sam, in every precise, beloved detail, an essence that vibrated with a truth beyond mere pattern. And with that recognition, a feeling took root at the very core of me, a quiet certainty that resonated more profoundly than any scientific term: *he'd seen me.*

Ascending the steps, I stole one final backward glance. Merely clouds now. Formless, unremarkable. Nevertheless, the sensation of connection persisted, a minuscule ember defying the surrounding emptiness.

"Having an existential moment with the atmosphere, freak?" Madison remarked sarcastically from her seat.

"Just... looking at stuff," I responded vaguely, lowering myself into a vacant spot near the rear.

Forehead pressed against the cool glass, I watched the world slide past. Storm clouds massed on the horizon, but patches of impossible blue persisted. For the first time since

I'd held the shovel, a question formed, as fragile as spun glass: What if 'gone' wasn't truly final? What if the world operated on rules more fundamental, stranger than I knew?

Logic screamed that buried meant buried, an undeniable end. Yet the rest of me—the part that recalled the comforting weight of his head on my knee, the unwavering, profound certainty that had shone from his eyes—clung to the smile in the clouds.

Maybe I was projecting. Or maybe... maybe Sam, somehow, had just waved hello.

CHAPTER 2:

WHISPERS AND WONDERS

The school hallway slammed into me—a cacophony of shouting voices, the clang of slamming lockers, the squeak of sneakers on linoleum, all vibrating under the headache-inducing hum of the fluorescent lights. Every sound felt too loud, every movement too fast. It was like walking into a high-speed foreign film after existing for days in the muted slow-motion of our grieving home, the lingering wonder of the smiling cloud the only real thing. I hunched my shoulders deeper, the backpack straps a familiar, unwelcome weight, and tried to navigate the jostling human current toward my locker.

"Thomas! Back among the living!" Josh Miller appeared suddenly, propped against my locker, basketball cradled under one arm. Madison's doing, undoubtedly.

"Sort of," I muttered, struggling with the combination, eyes fixed on the metal dial.

"Missing assignments are piling up. Armstrong threw a pop quiz. Ellis needed paper proposals yesterday."

He adjusted position, cutting off my retreat path. "Coach asked about your track status."

Track. The searing oxygen demand, the measured impact of each footfall, Sam waiting at practice's end, tongue lolling happily... a memory from someone else's life. The cloud image resurfaced in my mind—Sam running, unrestrained. "Undecided," I answered vaguely, exchanging textbooks. "Probably sitting out."

Josh frowned, his head tilted. "Because of your dog?" He sounded genuinely curious, which, instead of offering comfort, felt like a spotlight on a raw wound. "Madison said..."

Heat, sharp and sudden, flooded my face. I pictured Madison whispering the news, the pitying glances. Poor Will. The thought was a brand. My hand clenched on the locker door, and I slammed it shut—the clang a satisfying, metallic crack in the surrounding din.

"Gotta go," I bit out, shouldering past him before he could see the tremor in my hands.

"Hey, assignments—" Josh started, but I pushed past him into the flow.

Homeroom droned on—attendance, announcements. My gaze drifted to the window, desperately seeking some echo of the morning's miracle in the flat gray clouds, but found only an indifferent, ordinary sky. A fresh pang of emptiness tightened my chest.

Maybe I had imagined it.

"William?" Ms. Winters stood beside my desk as the room emptied. "A moment?"

My stomach plummeted. Math: C-minuses. She probably

wanted the work I'd missed. I waited as the last students filed out.

She perched on the desk before mine, arms crossed. Her usual sternness seemed softened. "I heard about your dog, William," she said directly. "I'm very sorry."

"Thanks," I mumbled, tracing a heart carved into my desk.

"I lost my dog when I was about your age," she continued, surprising me.

"A retriever, Chester. Couldn't focus for weeks." She paused until I met her eyes. "Grief fogs the brain. Makes it hard to care about algebra, doesn't it?"

"We'll sort out the missed work," she assured me. "One step at a time." Her tone shifted slightly. "But you will sort it out, William. That brain doesn't get a free pass." A hint of a smile touched her lips. "Now, off you go. And consider track when you're ready. Moving the body helps move the grief."

Her unexpected understanding, the blend of empathy and expectation, felt... grounding.

The morning dragged, each period a blur of voices I barely registered. I drifted through classes like a ghost, the simple act of holding a pencil or turning a page requiring an immense, deliberate effort. By lunch, my shoulders ached from the strain of trying to appear normal, my eyelids heavy as lead.

The cafeteria roared. Scanning the crowded tables, anxiety tightened its grip. Where to sit?

"Will! Over here!" Molly Chen waved from a table near the windows, gesturing to an empty seat beside her. A surprised laugh, small and rusty, almost escaped me. The knot of anxiety in my stomach seemed to loosen its grip, and my feet, which had felt rooted to the floor, suddenly found the will to move me toward her. Debate team kids, science clubbers—Aiden, Elena, Rafael.

"Hey, Will," Molly greeted, her smile open, lacking the pity I'd been dreading.

"How's it going?" Aiden asked casually.

"Okay," I said, and the word, to my surprise, didn't feel like a complete lie. Surrounded by their easy chatter and casual acceptance, a tiny piece of the usual me seemed to flicker back to life.

They talked—strategies, cafeteria pizza critiques, and Mr. Peterson's questionable hair dye. They included me without pressure. It felt... different. Easier.

"Are you doing the science fair?" Molly asked later. "Ms. Winters mentioned your interest in cloud formations."

I nearly choked. "She did?"

Molly nodded. "Said you asked some insightful questions. About predictive patterns?"

I remembered asking about the math behind cloud shapes. "Just curious," I mumbled.

"Not really fair material."

"You should reconsider," Rafael urged. "Plenty of time."

"Maybe." The idea sparked a flicker of my old self, the one who liked figuring things out.

The conversation moved on, but a flicker of comforting warmth remained. For a few minutes, life had felt almost normal.

The feeling didn't last. By seventh period, exhaustion weighed me down. Each teacher's query about assignments felt like another burden. When the final bell rang, I practically ran for the exit.

The bus ride was nearly silent. Lyn and Madison were absorbed in a magazine up front.

I slumped near the back, watching fields blur past. My thoughts returned to the morning cloud—its image so sharply etched in my memory, so undeniably Sam. Could it have been real? A message? Or ...grief?

The house stood empty. Mom's note on the counter: "Lyn @ soccer. Lasagna. Back by 6." Relief again—solitude felt safer than forced interaction. Sam's water bowl sat untouched by the fridge. The sight brought a dull ache, less sharp than before, more like a deep bruise.

I drifted through the rooms. Mom's Bible lay open in the living room, a verse marked:

"The Lord is close to the brokenhearted..." Her faith gave her an anchor I didn't have. I envied her certainty.

Sam in the Clouds

Outside, storm clouds gathered in the west, their underbellies a bruised purple. Yet directly overhead, the sky remained a stubborn, defiant blue, a single shaft of sunlight pouring down like a spotlight on the oak tree and the freshly turned earth of Sam's grave. It was that light, that insistent beam, that pulled at me, an almost physical tug in my chest, and before I knew it, my feet were carrying me out the door.

The grass felt cool and damp. A breeze rustled the oak leaves, a sound like hushed whispers. I sat beside the grave, tracing Mom's stone border.

"Hey, buddy," I whispered, the name a raw ache in my throat, the words catching there, half-formed with a desperate hope that felt utterly, ridiculously, necessary.

"Saw you this morning. I think I did, anyway. Your face. Smiling." The wind swirled leaves around my feet. "Was that you? Am I ...seeing things?"

Silence answered. Of course. A cold wave of disappointment washed over me, the rational part of my brain scoffing at my foolishness. And yet... That clear image from the morning, that specific Sam-ness, tightened its grip. It wasn't just any dog shape. It was he. The desperate yearning to believe, to have that connection be real, physically battled the cold logic that screamed it couldn't be.

I leaned back against the rough bark, face tilted up. Dark clouds advanced, but the column of golden sunlight over the oak held firm, defiant.

"William?"

Mom's voice made me jump. She stood at the edge of the yard, keys in hand. "What are you doing? It's about to pour."

I scrambled up. "Just thinking."

"The tension eased from her brow as her vision fell upon the grave, her eyes reflecting a deep understanding. "I talk to him too," she admitted, walking over. She slipped her arm through mine.

"I saw something," I confessed, the words rushing out. "This morning. Waiting for the bus. A cloud... It looked exactly like Sam. His face. Smiling."

Mom stopped, her hand still on my arm from when she'd comforted me about the grave.

She turned fully towards me, her earlier weariness vanishing, her eyes suddenly alight with an urgent focus. "Sam's face? Smiling?" she repeated, her voice a hushed breath.

I described it—the clarity, the light, how it felt like him. She listened, her brow tight with concentration, her lips parted slightly as if weighing every word.

"And look now," I urged, pointing to the persistent sunlight. "It's focusing right here, even with the storm."

"I see," she acknowledged.

"Do you think..." The question felt huge, fragile. "Does it mean anything?"

Sam in the Clouds

She watched the light for a long moment, her hand unconsciously tightening on my arm.

When she finally spoke, her voice was low but carried a new, resonant conviction. "I think," she said slowly, "love doesn't simply vanish, Will. And I think sometimes... signs are given. Ways to let us know they're at peace."

"But Sam wasn't..."

"He loved us," she interrupted gently. "Fiercely. That bond... it counts." She squeezed my arm. "Maybe God uses that love to send comfort. Not everyone sees."

"You've been looking too," I realized. "Photos, late nights."

A sad, genuine smile. "In my own way. But never anything this... specific."

The first raindrops hit—cold, heavy. But the sunlight persisted, catching the drops, making them glitter.

"Should go in," Mom murmured but stayed rooted.

"Wait," I whispered, transfixed.

Rain intensified, plastering hair to my forehead. Mom huddled closer. And then I saw it.

High against the storm clouds. Another shape. Sharper. Sam is sitting. Head tilted, listening intently, like he used to. So vivid it seemed etched against the tempestuous sky, defined as if traced by an artist's hand.

25

"Mom," I breathed, the word escaping on a rush of air I hadn't realized I was holding, my own heart leaping with a wild, terrified hope. "Look."

Her eyes tracked upward, following the direction I pointed. She blinked against the rain, then blinked again, her body going utterly still. A cold dread washed through me during that heart-stopping second—was it just me? Was I truly *losing* it? But then her breath hitched—a sharp, audible intake—and her fingers clamped down on my arm like a vise.

"Oh," she whispered, the word a fragile exhalation, her eyes wide and luminous with disbelief. "Oh, Will."

Frozen, rain forgotten, we stared. It wasn't just a shape. It was a presence. Benevolent.

Familiar. Yet infused with something more—a wisdom, a patience that transcended the dog we knew.

My mind, desperate for an anchor, scrabbled for explanations—pareidolia, tricks of grief-laden light, anything but the impossible truth unfolding. But then the cloud-Sam tilted his head higher, as if in direct response to my silent, frantic denials. The atmosphere between sky and earth seemed to thin, creating a visible disturbance that connected the clouds to the grave beneath the tree.

Instantly, where the connection touched the soil, the air filled with a scent I recognized more readily than my own reflection—clean dog, soap, that distinctive essence uniquely Sam. Every rational thought shattered. I could only stare, my own breathing suspended, a silent gasp trapped in my chest as the earth bulged slightly at the point of contact. A vivid green shoot emerged, unfurling with a speed that defied nature, developing before our very eyes as if a month of growth were compressed into heartbeats. Within moments, a complete flower materialized from the soil—pristine white petals spreading outward to reveal a rich golden center. The blossom positioned itself vertically, as though acknowledging the cloud formation that had called it into existence.

Mom gasped, her hand flying to her mouth, her eyes, already wide, now round with an almost terrified wonder. "William—are you—"

"You saw him too?" Mom asked, her voice barely audible as Max scratched at the door.

I could only nod, throat tight. Seeing signs was one thing. Seeing him...

The cloud's distinct outline began to blur and bleed into the surrounding grey, the light within it fading as the storm fully arrived. Rain poured, drenching us. Neither of us moved. Hammering heart. Racing mind.

"We should..." Mom started, unable to finish.

"Yeah." Go inside. Be normal. But "normal" had just evaporated with the rain.

Reluctantly, we turned. I glanced back—the white flower stood unharmed, untouched by the deluge.

"What does it mean?" I asked, my voice barely more than a

shaky whisper against the drumming rain under the porch roof.

Mom pushed her wet hair back, her eyes contemplative. "I don't know exactly. But Sam... he's telling us something."

"That he's okay?" The words tumbled out, a sudden surge of warmth spreading through my chest, momentarily pushing back the bone-deep chill of the rain. Hope, fragile but insistent, made my voice tremble slightly.

"Maybe." She studied me, a thoughtful, almost tender look in her eyes. "Or maybe... that we will be."

We stood dripping. The air smelled of wet earth and, unexpectedly, the delicate perfume of flowers that had no business blooming in the chill April air. Lightning flashed. For a split second, a distinctly Sam-shaped shadow seemed to stand beneath the oak, then vanished.

Mom opened the door. "Dry clothes," she murmured. "Then we talk."

Following her inside, shivers racking my body from a combination of the icy rain and the monumental shock of what we'd witnessed, I looked back through the rain-streaked window. Beneath the oak, the white flower stood defiant, unbowed by the downpour, a botanical impossibility persisting against meteorological reality. And as I watched it, something new, fragile yet insistent, began to unfurl within me—not joy, not yet, but a thread of warmth that eased the tightness in my chest. It was the first stirring of hope, a quiet, tremulous belief that perhaps Sam wasn't truly gone, that somehow, in some way, he remained. Still watching over us.

CHAPTER 3:

THE FLOWER THAT
SHOULDN'T EXIST

Mom handed me a towel the moment we stepped inside, water pooling around our soaked sneakers. Neither of us spoke. The drumming rain outside felt distant compared to the thunderous impossibility of what we'd witnessed. That white flower, blooming defiantly.

"You should change," Mom finally managed, her voice still tight with wonder. She ran the towel over her hair, damp curls clinging to her face. "I'll make hot chocolate."

Hot chocolate. Mom's standard remedy. The familiar offer felt absurdly normal after the afternoon's events. "Okay," I agreed, heading upstairs, leaving a trail of damp footprints.

In my room, I stripped off cold, wet clothes, pulling on dry jeans and a sweatshirt. My mind replayed the sequence: the light piercing the storm clouds, the green shoot erupting from the earth, and the petals unfurling in seconds. Impossible. Yet it happened. Mom saw it too.

Downstairs, she sat at the kitchen table, steam rising from two mugs. She'd also changed, but her hair remained damp, making her look younger, more vulnerable.

"Called your father," she said as I slid into my chair. "He's coming home."

That stopped me. Dad never left work early. Not for fevers, not for broken bones. "You told him? About—" My eyes involuntarily sought the rain-lashed window facing the backyard.

Mom tapped her mug. "Not everything. Just that something happened. Something we need to discuss." She took a careful sip. "Trying to explain that over the phone..." She didn't need to finish. Dad dealt in wood and nails, not inexplicable botany.

"What about Lyn?" I asked, wrapping cold hands around the warm ceramic.

"Maddy's mom is bringing her." Mom studied me. "Do you want to tell her?"

I pictured Lyn's probable scoffing and her accusations. But then, the image of her raw grief at Sam's burial surfaced— clutching his collar, tears streaming. She loved him fiercely, too. "Maybe," I said. "Let's see how Dad reacts first."

Mom gave a single, slow dip of her chin, her eyes still reflecting the awe and unease of what we'd just witnessed. We sat in a charged stillness, the rain drumming a relentless rhythm against the house. Sharing this extraordinary secret felt anchoring, less like my mind was fraying at the edges.

"I've been thinking," Mom began, her voice tentative at first, as if testing the words.
"Maybe we should talk to Pastor John."

My shoulders stiffened. Pastor John was kind, but this felt intensely personal. "Why?"

Mom traced the rim of her mug, her fingers trembling slightly. "He might offer perspective," she said, her tone gaining a quiet strength. "After my father passed, he helped me make sense of some... things I experienced."

"Things?" I leaned forward.

A wistful smile brushed her lips, though her eyes still held a shadow of that long-ago hurt and confusion. "I was about your age. Weeks after the funeral, I woke up smelling pipe tobacco—Grandpa's brand. So strong, Will, like he was right there in the room." Her gaze softened, drifting to a point beyond me, as if she could almost see him there now. "My mother couldn't smell it. Said I was imagining it."

"Were you?"

She shook her head firmly. "No. And Pastor John didn't think so either when I finally told him years later. He said, sometimes... those we love find ways to bridge the distance."

I turned this over. Bridge the distance. Like Sam? "So you think that's what this is?"

"I don't know," Mom admitted. "But what we saw wasn't ordinary. And when I can't explain things, spiritual guidance helps."

Headlights cut across the kitchen. The garage door rumbled. "Dad's home."

Mom straightened. "Remember," she murmured. "We know what we saw."

The back door opened, a gust of damp wind preceding Dad's solid frame. Rain slicked his jacket; boots dripped on the mat. His brow was etched with tight, worried furrows, eyes sharp as they scanned Mom, then me. Assessing.

"Marie?" He shed his wet jacket, hanging it. "What's going on? Taylor's crew is mid-truss."

Mom met him, hand on his arm. "Thank you for coming," she said simply. "Something happened. Something... significant."

His frown etched itself more sharply into his brow. "Are you okay? Lyn?"

"Everyone's fine," Mom assured him. "Physically. Please, Albert. Sit down."

Reluctantly, keeping his boots on—a clear sign of his unease—he allowed her to guide him to the table. He sat stiffly, forearms planted, eyes fixed on Mom. "Explain."

Mom glanced at me; I gave a slight nod. She turned back to Dad, taking a steadying breath. "Will and I were outside," she began. "By Sam's grave. And we saw something."

Dad waited, his shoulders visibly tense, hands flat on the table.

Mom described it—the second cloud, Sam sitting, the focused beam of light, and the flower blooming instantly.

She spoke calmly, factually, reporting, not pleading for belief.

When she finished, Dad hadn't moved a muscle. His eyes stayed locked on some point beyond Mom's shoulder, his face a stony mask, lips pressed into a thin, unreadable line.

"A flower," he repeated, his voice deliberately measured. "Emerged. Spontaneously. During a downpour."

"Not spontaneously," I corrected, my own voice small but determined, a knot of defensiveness tightening in my stomach. "From his grave. And it developed while we watched—right there."

Dad's attention shifted to me, his eyes narrowed, scrutinizing. "A flower," he echoed, the word heavy with a disbelief that felt like a physical weight between us.

Heat rushed to my cheeks, a hot flush of frustration. "Yes!" I said, perhaps too loudly, leaning forward in my chair. "After we both saw Sam's face formed in the clouds."

Dad let out a slow breath, rubbing his jaw, his gaze unwavering. "Will..."

"It wasn't imagination," I insisted, my voice rising, a desperate edge to it. "Mom saw it too! She was right there!"

"It's true, Albert," Mom affirmed, her voice low but steady. "I can't explain how, but it happened. The cloud... it was *him*. And the light, the flower—"

"Stop." Dad held up a hand, pinching the bridge of his nose.

He opened his eyes, weariness warring with something else—frustration? "Just... stop."

"Albert—" Mom started.

He shook his head. "Listen to yourselves," he said, his voice tight with exasperation.

"Cloud dogs? Instant flowers? This isn't..." He must have seen the hurt in my eyes, because the hard lines around his mouth eased a fraction. "Look, I know you're both hurting. We all are. But seeing things... inventing things..."

"It *wasn't* invented," I shot back, the force surprising me. "It's still there. Come see."

Dad's expression shifted, the frustration lines around his eyes softening into a look of pity that made my skin crawl and a fresh wave of hot anger surge through me—I would rather he yelled than look at me like I was broken.

"Son, plants don't work like that."

"So you think we're both just making it up, then?" I challenged, the words tight in my throat, the heat in my chest almost choking. "The exact same vision—the cloud, the light, a flower conjured from nowhere?"

"I think," Dad said, choosing words with deliberate care, "grief does strange things. Your mother hasn't slept properly. You've barely eaten. The mind can"—

Mom's head snapped up, her teacup clattering into its saucer as she placed it down with unintended force. Her eyes, moments before soft with shared wonder, now flashed with a protective fire. "Don't," she interrupted, her voice cutting through, sharp as tempered steel. "Don't diminish what we experienced, Albert."

His jaw clenched. "I'm not diminishing. I'm trying to be rational. To help—"

"Then just go look at it!" My voice cracked with the force of my conviction, and I shoved back from the table so hard my chair legs shrieked against the floor. "The flower is *right there*. Go look!"

Silence crackled between us. Thunder rolled overhead. Lightning flared, starkly illuminating the three of us locked in this standoff.

Dad's shoulders slumped almost imperceptibly. He blew out a long breath. "Fine," he conceded, the word heavy with reluctance. "Show me."

Mom grabbed the umbrella; I jammed my feet back into damp sneakers. Dad moved toward the back door like a man heading to a root canal. Immediately as he reached the handle, headlights swept the kitchen again. A car door slammed.

"Lyn," Mom murmured, umbrella half-open.

Dad paused. "Wait. We all go."

Part of me protested—wanted him to see it now, alone—but he was right. If this was real, *truly* real, we should all face it together.

The front door banged open. Lyn stomped in, soaked and muddy, soccer bag thudding to the floor. "Worst practice ever!" she declared. "Rain, drills, Coach is nuts—" She stopped short, taking in the scene: Mom poised with the umbrella, Dad by the back door, and me tense between them. Her eyes narrowed. "Okay, what? Why's everyone weird? Why's Dad home?"

We exchanged glances. I stepped forward. "Come see something," I told her. "Outside."

She scowled. "It's raining! I'm finally dry-ish!"

"It's important, Lyn," Mom urged, opening the umbrella fully.

Something in Mom's tone, maybe Dad's unexpectedly being there, made Lyn hesitate.

"Fine," she grumbled. "But this better be worth getting soaked again."

We went out together, Mom and Lyn under the umbrella, Dad and I bracing against the steady rain. Wet grass squelched. Mud clung to our shoes. As we neared the oak, my stomach twisted. Please be there.

And it was. Unbelievably, impossibly, there. White petals pristine, golden center vibrant against the dark, wet earth. Untouched by the downpour.

"There," I said, pointing.

Dad stopped, staring, his face a mask I couldn't read. Lyn peered out from under the umbrella, irritation dissolving into open curiosity.

"What is it?" she asked, stepping closer.

"Don't know," Mom answered softly. "Never seen one quite like it."

Dad crouched down, his gaze intense, scanning the flower and the surrounding soil without touching. "Wasn't here yesterday," he stated flatly.

"No," Mom confirmed. "It... appeared. While we were out here."

"Appeared how?" Lyn pressed, edging nearer, rain forgotten.

Mom and I locked eyes. How? "We saw Sam," I said, deciding directness was best. "In the clouds. Sitting. A light came down right here, and this just... grew. In seconds."

Lyn's eyebrows vanished under wet bangs. "No way."

"Yes, way," Mom responded.

Lyn looked to Dad for the verdict. He remained crouched, one hand hovering near the bloom, as if proximity might offer explanation or perhaps burn him. "Dad?"

Slowly, he straightened, rain plastering hair to his forehead. He looked from Mom to me, then his eyes returned to the flower, meticulously tracing its form, lingering on its flawless, otherworldly perfection. Skepticism still wrestled with a reluctant awe on his face. "I don't... understand this," he admitted finally, the words seeming pulled from him.

"It's highly unusual." High praise from Dad.

Vindication felt warm, but he quickly added, his voice attempting a familiar, dismissive tone, "Doesn't mean magic now. Could be some fast-growing fungus, a... a dormant seed triggered by lightning..." He ran a hand through his wet hair, his eyes darting away from ours, unable to hold a steady look, as his explanation faltered, the forced confidence draining from his voice.

"A fungus that smells like Sam?" Lyn asked, kneeling now, heedless of the mud. She sniffed cautiously. "It does! You know, after his bath? Clean, but still... him?"

I knelt beside her. She was right. Underneath the wet earth scent was something distinct, familiar—dog, shampoo, and that indefinable essence of Sam. "Yeah," I breathed. "It does."

Lyn reached out tentatively, finger hovering. "Can I...?" Receiving no objection, she gently brushed a fingertip against one perfect white petal.

Instantly, the flower reacted to Lyn's touch. The petal curved, a barely perceptible inclination toward her finger, while a subtle, thread-like tremor pulsed through the stem.

Lyn snatched her hand back as if shocked. "Whoa! Did you feel that? It's warm!"

I nodded, seeing Mom's eyes widen. Dad leaned closer, brow furrowed.

"Feel what?" he asked, his skepticism tinged with newfound curiosity.

"It's like..." Lyn struggled to explain, "like it has a heartbeat."

Mom reached out, her finger tentatively brushing against a petal. "There is something," she confirmed, her voice hushed with wonder. "A rhythmic pulsing."

Dad touched it cautiously, his expression transforming from doubt to puzzlement.

"Temperature difference," he murmured, though it sounded more like a question than an explanation. "Interesting."

Silence, heavy with unspoken possibilities, settled over us, punctuated only by the rain.

"I believe," Mom said eventually, her voice subdued yet resolute, "we should consult Pastor John. Tomorrow."

Dad offered no objection. He merely inclined his head once, attention fixed on the flower that contradicted horticulture, violated natural laws, and resisted rational explanation—the flower that responded to his daughter's touch and carried the unmistakable scent of the dog interred beneath it.

As we retraced our steps toward the house, my eyes drifted upward. The storm clouds parted, revealing a solitary star burning with unnatural clarity, positioned directly above the oak.

Scientific reasoning suggested coincidence. Yet standing there, drenched and cold, a different explanation surfaced:

divine confirmation.

Inside, the shared experience settled differently on each of us. Dad disappeared into the garage; the rhythmic thump-thump of his hammer suggested a need for solid, predictable work. Mom began dinner prep with sharp, focused movements. Lyn retreated upstairs, the muffled beat of her radio a distant pulse.

Exhaustion seeped into my bones—physical and emotional. The strain of grief, the reeling sense that the world had casually shrugged off its own rules right before my eyes, and the tension with Dad. Sitting at my desk, I found myself reaching for the untouched, leather-bound journal Grandma had given me. This needed documenting. This needed... containment.

Pen in hand, the words flowed surprisingly easily—the cloud face, Ms. Winters, Molly, the storm, the light, the grave-born flower, the glow, the scent. I described what happened, sticking to observations, the raw data of the inexplicable. Recording it felt calming, imposing a kind of order on the miraculous chaos.

A soft knock. "Will?" Lyn's voice, hesitant. "Can I come in?"

"Sure." I turned as she entered, also in pajamas. She hovered uncertainly.

"That flower," she started, picking at her sleeve. "You really think... *Sam*?"

I met her eyes. We hadn't truly talked in ages. But this wasn't our usual bickering. This was different. "I think so," I admitted. "That cloud this morning? It wasn't just *like* him, Lyn. It was him. Smiling."

She absorbed this slowly. "And Mom saw the second one? Sitting?"

"Yeah. The cloud, the light, the flower growing. We both saw it all."

Lyn looked down. When she looked up, vulnerability made her seem much younger. "I miss him," she said, the words barely a whisper. "So much."

"Me too." My throat constricted. "Keep thinking I hear his collar."

She hugged herself. "Last night, I dreamed he was on my bed, like during thunderstorms. It felt so real. Waking up was... awful."

A wave of shared sorrow washed over me, and all I could do was dip my chin in a slow, tight acknowledgment, unable to speak past the lump that had formed in my own throat. The dreams were the worst. Sam is bounding, waiting, and leaning against my leg.

Waking up always felt like the floor dropping out.

"Do you think..." Lyn hesitated. "Is he... okay? Pastor John says dogs don't have souls."

She rushed on, "But that feels wrong. Sam was smarter than most people."

Her question caught me off guard. Lyn, the believer, questioning doctrine? But after today... "I don't know about souls, exactly," I said carefully. "But I think he's somewhere. And he's trying to tell us he's okay. That we'll be okay."

Lyn considered this. "The clouds and the flower are messages?"

"Maybe. Or maybe just... reminders." I paused. "Pastor John didn't know Sam."

A small, watery smile. "Yeah. No one did. Not like us."

A comfortable silence settled between us, a fragile truce brokered by shared grief and shared wonder.

"Mom sent me," Lyn said eventually. "Dinner's almost ready."

"Okay. Thanks."

She turned and paused at the door. "Will? If you see him again, you'll tell me?" The plea was clear: Include me. My grief matters too.

"Promise," I said, and meant it.

A small, almost shy smile touched Lyn's lips, and the tense line of her shoulders seemed to relax a fraction. "Okay," she said, her voice softer now, seeming satisfied.

Then she left. I sat for another moment, the unexpected connection with Lyn feeling like another quiet, personal miracle in a day full of large ones. Maybe Sam was already working magic.

Dinner was subdued. The flower remained unmentioned, yet its presence dominated the space between us. Dad picked at his food, his eyes unfocused, seemingly fixed on something far beyond the kitchen walls. Mom maintained surface normalcy. An electric current of waiting hummed beneath the surface.

Afterward, we drifted to the living room together, an unusual occurrence. Dad watched the news on low volume. Mom held her Bible like a shield. Lyn sprawled with a magazine, pages turning unheeded. I sat by the window, peering out at the oak, a dark silhouette against the deepening twilight.

"Called Pastor John," Mom announced during a commercial. "He's coming tomorrow. Nine."

Dad looked up. "Church?"

"Associate Pastor Kevin's leading," Mom explained. "He thought this warranted his full attention."

Dad processed this, frowning slightly. "You told him...?"

"Enough," Mom said gently. "He sounded concerned. Interested. Not judgmental."

Dad made a noncommittal noise but didn't return to his paper.

"What will he say?" Lyn asked.

"Not sure," Mom admitted. "But he believes God works in

mysterious ways. He'll listen."

Conversation meandered, but the anticipation remained. Tomorrow might bring clarity or deeper mystery.

As bedtime approached, Mom made another unusual suggestion: "Let's check the flower. Together."

Dad looked startled. "Now? It's dark."

"Flashlights," Mom countered. "Rain stopped. I'd feel better knowing it's still there."

No one objected. We were all curious. Needing confirmation.

Dad found flashlights. We bundled up again. Outside, the night air was cool, washed clean. Stars blazed overhead. Our breath plumed. Flashlight beams danced across the wet lawn. Approaching the oak, that prickling awareness returned—not menacing, but expectant. Welcoming.

Dad's beam found it first. The white flower stood stark against the dark earth, impossibly bright. "Still there," Lyn breathed.

"And dry," Mom added, leaning in. "Dew all around, but the petals are bone dry."

Dad crouched, circling it with his light, his usual certainty visibly unsettled by the inexplicable evidence. "We'll see what the pastor makes of it," he said finally, straightening with a quiet, almost weary grunt.

As we turned back, a sound stopped us mid-stride. Unmistakable in the night stillness: the distinct jingle-jingle of metal tags against a collar. Followed by a soft, familiar woof.

Dad swept his flashlight beam across the darkness. Empty yard. Motionless branches.

Lyn's fingers tightened around mine, ice-cold. Mom's breath caught audibly.

"Did you hear—"

"Wind chimes," Dad asserted, the explanation coming too hastily. His beam continued probing the darkness. "Or a neighbor's dog. Sound carries at night."

Plausible explanations. Rational alternatives. But huddled together, retracing our steps, none of us truly believed it was only the wind. We'd received another message. Another reminder. Love bridges even the ultimate distance.

Later, staring at the ceiling, glow-in-the-dark stars faint overhead, the day replayed.

Clouds. Light. Flower. Glow. Scent. Jingle. Bark. Evidence stacked against logic. Science offered no refuge here. What was this?

Sleep remained a distant shore. As exhaustion finally began to pull me under, a single, insistent thought surfaced: This isn't just about comfort, is it? There's a reason. A purpose for Sam... for us. The question wasn't unsettling but vast, opening into the starry expanse of my drifting mind, leading me into dreams where gardens bloomed under an otherworldly starlight, their luminous flowers echoing the one that had so defied logic beneath our oak. And through them, a white dog ran, always right ahead, glancing back as if to say, Keep coming. There's more to see.

CHAPTER 4:

THE PASTOR'S VISIT

M orning arrived with startling clarity after yesterday's tempest. Bright shafts of sunlight sliced through my blinds, illuminating dancing dust motes like tiny, random galaxies. For a disorienting second, everything felt normal—then memory flooded back. The cloud.

The flower. The jingle in the dark.

I sat bolt upright. Pastor John. He was coming today.

Downstairs, the house hummed with a nervous energy unlike any Sunday morning I could remember. Mom moved with brisk, distracted motions—tidying already clean surfaces, checking cinnamon rolls baking in the oven, their sweet scent filling the kitchen.

"Special breakfast?" I asked, eyeing the rolls.

"Thought we could all use something nice before Pastor John arrives," Mom replied, adjusting the timer. "He's only coming to talk, not for a meal. But I always think better with cinnamon in the air." She offered a small smile. "And we have plenty to discuss."

Dad, surprisingly, sat at the kitchen table, not out on a job site. Mug cradled between his hands, he scanned the paper, attempting casualness, but his shoulders remained tight beneath the worn flannel.

"Morning, I offered, sliding into my chair.

He acknowledged me with a brief nod, his eyes skimming over me. "Sleep okay?"

"Better than I expected." True, actually. The dreams, though vivid, had left me feeling oddly rested.

Mom placed orange juice before me. "Pastor John will be here in forty-five minutes," she announced, glancing at the clock. "Where's Lyn?"

"Shower," Dad replied. "Auditioning for 'Eye of the Tiger,' sounds like." A ghost of amusement touched his voice, the first in days. Lyn's shower concerts were infamous.

Sam used to sit outside the door, head cocked, occasionally adding his own mournful howl. The memory brought a pang, gentler this time. I almost smiled.

"Have you checked... it?" I asked.

Mom paused, arranging fruit. "Yes. Still there. Still... exactly the same."

"Exactly the same meaning..." Dad prompted, skepticism audible but slightly less sharp than yesterday.

"Dry," Mom explained, setting the platter down firmly. "Pristine. Like it's under glass, or... I don't know, Albert. Protected. You saw it."

Dad pushed his coffee cup an inch, then another, his gaze fixed on the tabletop as if the answers were etched in the wood grain. He finally looked up, a slow breath escaping him. "I saw a flower blooming out of season," he conceded, his voice carefully neutral.
"Unusually resistant to weather. That doesn't mean—"

"It glowed, Dad," I interrupted. "When Lyn touched it. We all saw that." The oven timer chimed, a timely interruption.

Dad focused on his coffee while Mom retrieved the cinnamon rolls. Their warmth filled the kitchen, pulling at memories—birthdays, Christmas, the day we brought Sam home.

"So, what's the plan?" Dad asked after a moment, looking mainly at Mom as she served the rolls. "Pastor John arrives, and we march him out back to see a supposedly miraculous flower."

Mom set a plate in front of me, the sweet, sticky scent momentarily distracting from the tension. "I thought we'd explain what happened over coffee. Then, yes, show him." Her eyes locked with Dad's across the table as she passed him a roll. "Unless you're embarrassed, our pastor might think your wife and son encountered something... beyond the ordinary."

We ate quickly, the rolls delicious despite the strained atmosphere. By the time we'd finished and cleared our plates, Lyn had joined us, and the doorbell was minutes away from ringing.

Dad flinched, his jaw tightening for a moment before he

spoke. "That's not fair, Marie," he said, his voice low and tight. "I'm only trying..."

"To find a logical explanation?" she countered. "There isn't one, Albert. Not for all of it."

I sank lower, uncomfortable with the friction crackling between them. They rarely argued openly.

Footsteps pounded downstairs. Lyn bounced into the kitchen, hair damp, wearing her favorite purple sweater and rip-free jeans—her version of dressing up. Her eyes widened at the rolls. "Whoa, fancy. Is Pastor John staying to eat?"

"Thought something special would be nice," Mom replied, tension easing slightly as she served Lyn. "After everything."

Lyn leaned forward. "Think he'll want to study the flower? Like, scientifically?"

"He's a spiritual leader, Lyn, not a botanist," Dad pointed out, though his tone lacked its usual dismissal of church matters. "He'll offer... perspective."

"He might have questions," Mom added, placing rolls on our plates. "About what we experienced, felt. Be honest, even if it sounds..." She searched for the word.

"Impossible?" Lyn supplied.

"Unconventional," Mom corrected, a flicker of a smile crossing her face.

We ate mostly in silence, the clink of forks the loudest sound. Nervousness gnawed at my stomach. What if Pastor John thought we were making it up? Dismissed it? Said it was wrong to believe Sam might still be near?

The doorbell chimed, its sound slicing through the tense hush of the room.

"He's early," Mom noted, wiping her hands and smoothing her hair. "I'll get it."

Dad stood too, adjusting his shirt and clearing his throat. Lyn and I exchanged wide-eyed glances. We stayed put as Mom's footsteps receded, the door opened, and her warm greeting drifted back.

"John, thank you for coming. Please, come in."

Pastor John's deep, calm voice responded. "Marie. Good to see you. Your call gave me much to consider."

Their voices neared. Pastor John appeared, his tall frame filling the doorway. Silver streaked his dark hair; instead of his Sunday suit, he wore casual khakis and a blue button-down. His eyes, sharp yet kind, moved deliberately across the room, resting briefly on each of us.

"Albert," he said, extending a hand to Dad. "Good to see you."

"You too, John," Dad responded, his tone carefully neutral. "I appreciate you making time."

Pastor John turned to Lyn and me, his smile genuine. "And

Lyn, William. How are you both holding up?"

"Okay," Lyn answered quickly. "Better since the flower."

His eyebrows lifted slightly. "Ah yes, the flower. Part of why I'm here, I gather." His gaze shifted to me. "William, your mother mentioned you noticed something unusual first? In the clouds?"

All eyes turned to me. My throat went dry. I'd known him my whole life—baptisms, youth group, occasional dinners. But describing this felt different, raw, and exposed.

"Maybe we should sit in the living room," Mom suggested smoothly, sensing my discomfort. "It's a bit of a story."

Pastor John nodded. "Excellent idea. And perhaps some coffee? It was an early start arranging things for Associate Pastor Kevin."

The small talk eased the tension as we relocated. Dad and Pastor John took the armchairs; Mom, Lyn, and I claimed the couch. Mom handed the pastor a steaming mug before he turned back to me, attention focused but gentle.

"Now then," he invited. "Tell me what you saw, William."

I described yesterday afternoon—the second cloud, with Sam sitting there as plain as day, the beam of focused light, and then the flower... how it had erupted from the raw earth of his grave in mere seconds, perfect and fully formed, as if conjured. Pastor John listened intently, expression unreadable, offering neither judgment nor immediate belief.

"And last night," I finished, "we all heard it. Sounds like Sam's collar tags. His bark. But nothing was there."

Silence settled. Pastor John sipped his coffee slowly, his look moving thoughtfully between us. "Marie, Albert," he said finally. "You both witnessed this flower appear?"

"I did," Mom confirmed. "Exactly as Will described. The light, the growth—all of it."

Dad shifted in his chair. "I didn't see it appear," he admitted. "But I saw the flower itself afterward. It's... there. And staying dry in the rain is peculiar."

"And the glow?" Pastor John inquired. "When did Lyn touch it?"

"We all saw that," I confirmed. Dad gave a reluctant, almost imperceptible nod.

"Fascinating," Pastor John murmured, setting his mug down. "And you connect these occurrences to Sam? Your dog?"

The clinical term felt wrong. "Not just any dog," I corrected, needing him to see what I meant. "Sam was... different."

Pastor John focused fully on me, a flicker of recognition in his eyes. "Different how, William?"

The question opened a floodgate. I described Sam—not simply his habits, but his presence. How he seemed to take in full conversations. How he simply knew when someone was upset, offering silent comfort. The unnerving

53

intelligence in his eyes. The feeling he was more than a pet, almost a… guardian.

When I fell silent, Pastor John watched me, and for the first time, I saw neither pity nor skepticism in his expression. Instead, a profound empathy seemed to bridge the space between us, a look that mirrored my own conviction about Sam's uniqueness. "You know," he said, "I had a dog once. When I was about your age. A collie mix named Bishop."

This was unexpected. He rarely shared personal stories.

"Bishop was extraordinary," he continued, his eyes unfocusing, lost for a moment in the soft haze of memory. "A wisdom about him I've never encountered since. My father joked, Bishop understood theology better than most seminary students."

Lyn leaned forward. "What happened to him?"

A shadow crossed the pastor's face. "He died saving me. I wandered too close to thin ice on a pond. Bishop pulled me back but fell in himself." He paused, the decades-old pain still evident. "I was inconsolable. Until about three weeks later."

"That loss led me down a path I hadn't anticipated," Pastor John continued, his voice taking on a more personal tone. "Before I tell you about those flowers, there's something you should know about my background."

He paused, clearly considering how much to share. "After Bishop died and what followed, I became fascinated with spiritual connections that transcend death. In college, I didn't only study theology—I specifically sought out comparative religion courses examining how different traditions understand the continuity of bonds beyond physical death."

"My professors were concerned about my 'unhealthy fixation' until Dr. Reynolds recognized what I was actually seeking. He arranged for me to spend a year in Tibet after graduation, studying with Buddhist monks who had preserved ancient understandings about the connections between worlds."

Dad recrossed his legs, the slight scrape of his shoe the only sound in the room, but his look, which had been skeptical, now fixed on Pastor John with a new, questioning intensity.

"At the monastery, I met Master Rinpoche, who taught that certain souls—including those of animals—serve as guides between realms of existence. The monastery had an old temple dog, white with one dark ear, who the monks believed could perceive visiting spirits and would often lead people to places they needed to be before they knew they needed to go there."

"Like Sam did with us," Lyn whispered.

A gentle smile touched Pastor John's lips as he inclined his head toward Lyn. "Very similar, yes. My experiences there helped me understand what had happened with Bishop in a broader spiritual context. When I returned home and eventually entered seminary, I kept most of these insights private. Western theological frameworks rarely address the way such profound bonds can bridge different planes of existence in depth, particularly regarding animals."

But over forty years of ministry," he continued, his warm, thoughtful eyes moving from face to face, drawing us all into his confidence, "I've encountered countless stories of continued bonds that defy conventional explanation. These experiences aren't contrary to faith—they may be the very essence of it: love that transcends physical boundaries."

He settled back slightly.

"Walking home through Alderman's Woods—a place forbidden after Bishop was gone—my eyes fell upon a sight that, to this day, I can scarcely believe." He leaned forward slightly. "Near the old central oak. A perfect circle of white flowers. Blooming. In February. Through snow."

My skin prickled. "Like ours?"

"Perhaps. Smaller, like snowdrops, but not quite. Dozens of them. But yes, blooming where they shouldn't, when they shouldn't." Pastor John met my eyes. "I knew, instantly, they were from Bishop. A message."

Saying what?" Dad asked, his voice a beat too quick, a slight frown still etched between his brows even as he leaned forward almost imperceptibly.

A rueful smile touched Pastor John's lips. "That's the question. At the time, I thought he was letting me know he was at peace. That I shouldn't worry.' He paused, his expression deeply thoughtful. "Later, I came to believe it might have been... more."

"More how?" Mom prompted.

He chose his words carefully. "In seminary, we study the nature of souls, divine messengers, and the ways God communicates. Christianity has traditions of signs and wonders, though modern churches often focus elsewhere." He gestured broadly. "Some might find my views unorthodox, but decades of ministry suggest God's relationship with creation is more complex, more beautiful, than our systems allow. Love—God's essential nature—doesn't create boundaries where none need exist."

"So you think these signs... from Sam... could be real?" I pressed, needing his validation.

"Yes, William," he replied without hesitation. "I believe what you're experiencing may be entirely real."

Dad sat forward, hands clasped. "Pastor John, how do you square this"—he" gestured vaguely toward the backyard—"with" theology? Dogs having souls? Communicating after death?"

Pastor John considered Dad's question thoughtfully. "Formal theology focuses on human salvation, Albert. Animals are part of creation but viewed differently." He looked toward the window facing the oak. "But life teaches us things seminary doesn't cover.
Scripture itself hints at more—animals in visions of heaven, included in God's covenant.
Christ is called redeemer of all creation."

He moved to his bookshelf, fingers trailing along leather bindings before selecting a weathered volume. "The church fathers themselves debated this question. St. Francis of Assisi spoke to animals as fellow creatures of God. And some more recent thinkers, whose stories of other worlds you might know, William, have beautifully explored how animals might participate in eternity through their relationship with humans, sharing in our immortality through love."

"That's what this feels like," I ventured, finding unexpected courage in his openness.

"Like Sam is... continuing... because of our connection."

Pastor John nodded, returning to his seat with the book. "The theological term would be 'participation'—one being sharing in the nature or experience of another. Humans participate in God's nature through grace. Perhaps animals, in their way, participate in human spiritual nature through the bonds of love."

"But isn't that wishful thinking?" Dad asked, though his tone sought understanding rather than dismissal. "Seeing what we want to see because we miss him?"

"That's always a valid question, Albert," Pastor John acknowledged. "Discernment is essential. But consider the nature of the experiences you've described—the specific cloud formations, the flower's unusual properties, and the scent associated with Sam.

These aren't vague feelings or impressions, but concrete, shared perceptions. Multiple witnesses experiencing the same phenomena suggests something beyond mere psychological projection."

He opened the book, showing us an illustration of medieval monks accompanied by faithful dogs. "Throughout Christian tradition, profound spiritual experiences have often included sensory elements—scents, sounds, and visual manifestations. These aren't considered less real for being supernatural. Rather, they represent moments when the veil between worlds grows momentarily thin."

"So you believe Sam's... spirit... could actually be guiding us?" Mom asked, her voice hopeful yet seeking confirmation.

"I believe," Pastor John replied, choosing his words with careful precision, "that love itself is the bridge. The bonds we form, especially ones as deep as you describe with Sam, may be allowed to continue to communicate in ways that defy easy explanation. God uses many messengers."

"Angels," Dad supplied, his engineering mind struggling to categorize these experiences.

Pastor John smiled gently. "'Angel' simply means 'messenger,' Albert. Perhaps, in that sense. I wouldn't presume to categorize it precisely. But profound spiritual connections happen. And perhaps," he continued, his thoughtful eyes meeting each of ours in turn, "there's wisdom in accepting the comfort and guidance being offered without requiring complete theological explanation. Faith often begins by recognizing a blessing before understanding it fully."

The idea settled over us—permission to accept Sam's continuing presence as a gift rather than a puzzle. For the first time since the burial, I felt a weight lifting. Not because

I'd found definitive answers, but because I'd discovered I wasn't alone in asking the questions. Even within the structured framework of formal religion, there was space for the miraculous, the unexplainable—the continuing bonds of love that transcended ordinary understanding.

Dad leaned forward further. "Are you suggesting our dog is some kind of... angel?"

A low, amiable chuckle rumbled in Pastor John's chest. "'Angel' simply means 'messenger,' Albert, as I said. And while I wouldn't presume to categorize Sam precisely, such deep bonds certainly open pathways we don't fully comprehend."

Pastor John leaned forward, his expression thoughtful. "William, there's something else you should know. Your experiences have attracted attention beyond our community."

"What kind of attention?" Dad asked, immediately protective.

"Scholarly interest, primarily. Dr. Eleanor Reeves from State University contacted me last week. She leads their parapsychology department."

"Parapsychology?" Mom echoed, sounding uncertain.

"The scientific study of phenomena that appear to transcend conventional physical explanation," Pastor John clarified. "Dr. Reeves has spent thirty years documenting what she calls 'threshold experiences'—occurrences similar to what you're describing with Sam."

This was unexpected. "A scientist is interested in Sam's... manifestations?" The idea that our deeply personal experiences might have broader significance hadn't occurred to me.

"Very interested," Pastor John confirmed. "She's been cataloging similar cases for decades—instances where bonds between humans and animals appear to continue beyond physical death. Your documentation, particularly the flower's properties and the recurring cloud formations, represents what she calls 'exceptional evidence.'"

"What does she want?" Dad's tone remained cautious.

"To conduct a small, respectful study if you're willing. Temperature sensors, specialized cameras, atmospheric monitoring—all unobtrusive. She believes your experiences may help bridge scientific understanding and spiritual phenomena."

Mom and Dad exchanged meaningful glances. "What do you think, Pastor John?" Mom asked. "Would this be... appropriate?"

He considered carefully. "I believe understanding more about these connections helps us appreciate their significance. Dr. Reeves approaches her work with both scientific rigor and profound respect. This could help others experiencing similar phenomena feel less alone."

"And legitimize what we're seeing," Dad added, surprising me with his interest.

"Precisely," Pastor John agreed. "Science and faith need

not be adversaries. At their best, they're different languages describing the same underlying reality."

The possibility that Sam's guidance might have significance beyond our family felt both overwhelming and somehow right. Like another layer of purpose unfolding.

"We should think about it," Mom suggested. "After we confirm what's happening with the trust."

"Of course," Pastor John agreed. "No rush. Dr. Reeves understands the sensitivity." He smiled gently. "But I thought you should know—what you're experiencing resonates beyond your family. It may have meaning for many others."

"So we're not crazy?" Lyn asked bluntly.

"No, Lyn, I don't think you're crazy." Pastor John's smile broadened, then turned serious again. "I would, however, very much like to see this flower."

Mom rose immediately. "Of course. It's beneath the oak."

We filed outside into the bright morning. Pastor John walked beside me. "Your mother mentioned you were particularly close to Sam," he said.

I shrugged, uncomfortable. "We all loved him."

"Of course. But sometimes certain bonds are conduits." He paused as we reached the oak. "William, in my experience, unusual spiritual events often center on those most open— perhaps unknowingly—to perceiving beyond the ordinary veil."

Before I could ask what he meant, Mom called out, "Here it is, John," gesturing to the pristine white flower defying the damp earth around Sam's grave.

Pastor John approached deliberately, kneeling despite his khakis. His expression transformed from professional interest to authentic wonder as he examined the perfect petals, the golden center, and the inexplicable dryness. "Extraordinary," he breathed, leaning closer without making contact. "Resembles a lily, but the structure... entirely unique." He looked up at Mom. "May I?"

She gave permission. We watched intently as he gently extended one finger.

The flower didn't merely react this time. It transformed. The white petals became momentarily transparent, revealing intricate inner structures usually hidden. A faint musical note—almost like a crystalline hum—emanated from the bloom as it vibrated at a frequency we could both hear and feel. The phenomenon lasted several seconds before gradually subsiding.

Pastor John withdrew his hand, surprised but not fearful. "Well," he said after a moment, unmasked amazement in his voice. "That's certainly... confirmation."

"It glowed when I touched it," Lyn offered. "But different. More like a heartbeat."

"This was more like... captured sunlight," Pastor John mused, rising. "Yes, exactly." He turned to face us all, brushing soil from his knee. "I believe this is genuine. A spiritual manifestation. A sign."

Dad's jaw worked silently for a moment. "A sign of *what*?"

"That," Pastor John said, his gaze steady, "is what we need to discern. Signs like these often point toward purpose. A message. Sometimes, a mission." He addressed all of us.

"Was Sam particularly connected to any place? A cause? Something perhaps unfinished?"

Mom and Dad exchanged puzzled looks. But a memory surfaced—Dad lifting Sam from that cardboard box at the shelter, the overwhelming noise, Sam looking so new and fragile and utterly uncertain until Dad handed him to me.

"The animal shelter," I said.

"Maple Street Animal Rescue. Where we got him."

Pastor John's expression quickened with interest. "A shelter. Significant. Any connection since?"

Dad shook his head. "Donation when we adopted him. Years ago."

"We should visit," Mom suggested, turning to Dad. "See how they are. Make another donation? In Sam's memory?"

To my surprise, Dad didn't immediately dismiss it. He stared at the flower for a long moment, then his attention shifted, his eyes moving deliberately from Mom to Lyn and finally to me, a flicker of something unreadable in their depths. He scrubbed a hand over his jaw, then let out a slow breath that seemed to carry some of his resistance with it. "I suppose," he said, the word drawn out, as if tasting its unfamiliarity, "given everything... that seems appropriate."

"An excellent starting point," Pastor John approved warmly. "Revisiting Sam's origins might clarify the purpose behind these signs."

A gust of wind swirled leaves and pollen around us. For an instant—so brief I blinked—the shifting shadows on the ground seemed to coalesce beside the flower into a familiar, four-legged shape before dissolving.

Pastor John saw it too. His eyes widened almost imperceptibly. He said nothing, but his expression firmed with conviction.

"I should let you get on with your Saturday," he said after a moment. "But please, stay in touch. Call me after you visit the shelter."

"Of course," Mom agreed readily. "And thank you, John. For... believing us."

"Faith requires openness to mystery, Marie." His smile included us all. "Sometimes God speaks in stillness. And sometimes, perhaps, through the enduring love of a dog."

As we walked back, Pastor John fell into step beside me again. "William," he said, "I'd be interested in hearing more about your experiences. Could you stop by my office next week?"

The invitation was unexpected. "Um, sure," I agreed. "Why me?"

He studied me for a moment. "Because you saw him first. And because..." He paused.

"Let's just say I recognize something in your description of Sam and in these events.

Something I've encountered before, in different forms."

With that cryptic remark, he rejoined my parents, leaving me pondering as we went inside. What did he recognize?

Pastor John declined more coffee, needing to check on things before the noon baptism.

When Dad shook his hand, the gesture was firm, his gaze direct and thoughtful—a clear departure from the guarded neutrality he'd shown when the pastor first arrived.

"Call anytime, day or night," Pastor John told us at the door. "Spiritual experiences can be overwhelming. You're not alone."

"After he left, we gathered in the kitchen, the energy in the room palpably lighter. Mom cleared dishes, a low, contented hum vibrating in her throat. Dad leaned against the counter, arms crossed, but his shoulders, usually so tense, were relaxed.

"So," Lyn broke the silence, "when are we going to the animal shelter?"

Dad checked his watch. "Nearly eleven. Need to swing by Millfield first." He glanced at

Mom. "Early afternoon?"

"Perfect," Mom agreed, pleasure warming her face at his proactive tone. "I'll call ahead."

"Can I bring my birthday money?" Lyn asked. "To donate?"

Mom smiled, resting a hand on Lyn's hair. "That's very thoughtful."

"I've got savings too," I offered, wanting to honor Sam as well. "From mowing lawns."

Dad regarded us both, pride mixing with something more complex. "Tell you what," he said. "Whatever you kids contribute, I'll match. For Sam."

The name, spoken without awkwardness, hung in the air. For Sam. Acknowledgment.

Progress.

As Dad headed out and Mom picked up the phone, Lyn turned to me, serious. "Think it'll happen again? Seeing Sam?"

"Don't know," I answered honestly. "But Pastor John seemed to think there's more to come. A purpose."

Lyn responded slowly. "I want to be there next time. I want to see him. Like you and Mom did."

"I promised," I reminded her, feeling surprisingly little irritation. Her insistence felt different today. Natural.

"Telling isn't seeing," she pointed out with flawless twelve-year-old logic.

Mom returned from her call, keys in hand. "All set. Martha says we can come by this afternoon, around three. That gives your father time to wrap up at the Millfield site."

"Perfect," I said, glancing at the clock. It was barely eleven. "I'll get my homework done before then."

The next few hours crawled by, each minute stretching like taffy. I tried focusing on algebra but ended up staring out the window, watching clouds for shapes that never quite formed. Lyn paced between her room and the kitchen, checking the clock every fifteen minutes. Even Mom seemed restless, organizing kitchen drawers that hadn't bothered her yesterday.

By two-thirty, we were all ready—changed into clean clothes, donation money tucked into wallets, hovering near the front door. Dad pulled into the driveway right on time, freshly showered from his morning at the site. Within minutes, we were backing out of the driveway.

"Kids!" Mom called from the front seat. "Shelter's open till five. We'll have plenty of time to look around."

"Coming!" Lyn yelled back, then added to me in a lower voice, "Wear your hoodie with the big pockets."

"Why?"

She rolled her eyes. "In case we find anything important there, dummy. Something connected."

Her certainty—that we would find something, that this visit held significance beyond nostalgia or donation—caught me by surprise. Was she right? Was there more to discover?

Heading upstairs, I glanced out toward the oak. The white flower stood, a small beacon against the dark earth. For a moment, I thought I saw a flicker nearby—something white, dog-sized—but it vanished with a blink. Trick of light. Or maybe... maybe Sam was guiding us toward something we didn't yet understand. Either way, Lyn had a point.

Whatever awaited me at Maple Street, I wanted to be ready. I wished I knew what for.

CHAPTER 5:

MAPLE STREET MEMORIES

Maple Street Animal Rescue looked unchanged, tucked away on the edge of town like a forgotten memory. Faded blue trim clung to the single-story building; the gravel parking lot remained a minefield of potholes. Dad navigated them carefully, the truck bouncing, jostling loose fragmented images from seven years ago: a deafening wall of barks, the sharp tang of disinfectant layered over kibble and damp fur, and my own six-year-old heart thrumming as Dad lifted a cute white puppy from a cardboard box.

"Doesn't look like much has changed," Dad commented, his voice flat as he eased the truck beside a dented white van bearing the faded letters "MSAR."

"Expecting a five-star resort?" Mom asked, unclipping her seatbelt. Dad cut the engine, the ensuing silence amplifying the shelter's worn appearance. He gave a brief, almost imperceptible shake of his head, more resigned than critical, before shrugging.

"Seven years. You'd think they might've found funds to fix that leaky roof." His eyes drifted upward, and there was no mistaking the state of the tired, haphazardly patched shingles.

Above the entrance, the weathered wooden sign, "MAPLE

STREET ANIMAL RESCUE," had letters bleached pale by sun and rain.

"Can we go?" Lyn bounced in the backseat, vibrating with an energy starkly contrasting our visit's somber undercurrent. "Want to see the dogs!"

The truck doors had barely thumped shut before Lyn was a blur, halfway to the shelter entrance. "Lyn!" Mom's voice snagged her just shy of the door. As Lyn reluctantly paused, I stepped onto the gravel, the spring air hitting me—a wave of damp earth and sharp pine from the nearby woods, all cut through with something raw and achingly unforgettable: the close, clustered scent of fur, fear, and a fragile, flickering hope that was uniquely animal shelter.

A bell suspended inside the door jingled as Dad pushed it open. The sound—achingly precise in its echo of Sam's tags hitting his water bowl—stopped us cold. Lyn froze mid-stride. Dad's hand paused on the knob. Mom drew a sharp, stifled breath. For a stretched second, we stood suspended in the doorway, ambushed by an echo.

"Be right with you!" a warm, slightly breathless voice called out, breaking the spell.

The reception area felt smaller than I remembered. Linoleum worn down to gray along common paths. Bulletin boards plastered with photos of beaming families, handwritten thank-yous, and flyers for long-past bake sales. A half-empty donation jar sat beside informational pamphlets.

A door behind the counter opened. A woman emerged,

71

wiping her hands on a towel tucked into her waistband. Sixties, maybe older, short silver hair framing a face etched with kindness and worry lines. Her blue polo, embroidered "MSAR," bore faint stains.

Reading glasses dangled from a beaded chain.

"Welcome to Maple Street," she greeted, eyes crinkling. "I'm Martha Wilson, shelter director. Thinking about adding to the family?"

Mom stepped forward. "Actually, no. I called earlier. Marie Thomas. We adopted our dog here years ago. We wanted to... visit."

A wave of recognition smoothed the worry lines around Martha's eyes, and her expression warmed. "Of course, Marie! I remember our chat." Her eyes, alight with recollection, traveled warmly over us, pausing on Dad. "You must be Albert. And these two... goodness."

Dad looked surprised. "You worked here seven years ago?"

Martha chuckled, a rich, genuine sound. "Running this place nearly twenty years, dear. Had more help back then. Mostly me and volunteers now." She leaned over the counter, addressing Lyn and me. "So, which lucky soul became a Thomas?"

"Sam," I answered, the name feeling both heavy and vital. "White dog, medium. One ear flopped more."

Something flickered in Martha's expression—not just recollection, but resonance.

"Sam," she repeated softly, her eyes unfocusing for a moment as if seeing him clearly in her memory. "Oh, I remember Sam. Quite the character. An extraordinary animal."

I saw Dad, who had been examining a faded 'adopt-a-thon' poster, turn his head sharply at Martha's words. A muscle twitched in his jaw, just once, and the tight set of his shoulders seemed to lessen almost imperceptibly before he looked away, feigning interest in a chew toy display.

Her word choice—extraordinary—echoed Pastor John's description of Bishop.

Coincidence? "You remember him specifically?" I pressed, leaning forward. "After all the dogs?"

Martha tilted her head, regarding me with new interest. "Some just stick, young man. Sam was one. Smarter than he had any right to be. It seemed like he understood every word." Her gaze shifted between my parents. "Is he... still with you?"

Mom shook her head, her voice hollow. "He passed. Last week. Cancer."

"Oh, I'm so very sorry," Martha said, genuine sympathy in her eyes. "Losing them is the hardest part. Especially the special ones." She hesitated. "Is that why you're here?

Saying goodbye?"

An awkward beat stretched. Explaining the flower, the clouds, and Pastor John's counsel—it felt too much, too fast.

Dad cleared his throat, stepping forward slightly. "We wanted to make a donation in Sam's memory. And the kids were curious where he came from." It wasn't the whole truth, but it served. Lyn shot me a frustrated look, vibrating with untold stories, but I gave a subtle headshake. Not yet.

"That's very generous," Martha replied, though I sensed a flicker of disappointment, as if she knew there was more. "We appreciate any support. Things have been... tight."

"Tight how?" Mom asked gently.

Martha sighed, polishing her glasses on the towel, the gesture seeming to buy her a moment.

"Financially," she admitted, her voice low. "Donations are down, surrenders are up. It seems everyone is struggling these days. And this old building... it's struggling right alongside us. It needs repairs we simply can't afford. Now, the county is requiring significant facility upgrades for us to keep our license past the summer."

She continued, ticking items off on her fingers, each one a fresh wave of overwhelm.

"New kennel flooring—the old concrete is so cracked and pitted, no amount of scrubbing truly gets it clean, and it's a constant worry for keeping the animals healthy. Then there's the drainage, which is a nightmare, and the ventilation system is archaic.

All absolutely necessary, vital for the animals, but the costs are staggering. Our fundraising efforts, bless the hearts of those who've helped, haven't even scratched the surface."

As Martha spoke, I saw Mom's hand instinctively go to the thin gold cross at her throat, her fingers tracing its familiar shape. Her expression, already etched with sympathy, deepened into a look of profound concern, her gaze fixed on Martha with an almost painful empathy. She made a nearly inaudible sound, a sigh that seemed to carry the weight of Martha's burden.

"Serious upgrades?" Dad asked then, his contractor instincts clearly kicking in.

Martha sighed, the sound heavy with the weight of her responsibilities. 'It starts with the kennel flooring,' she explained, her eyes losing focus for a moment, as if she were mentally walking through the worn-out runs. "The old concrete is so cracked and pitted, no amount of scrubbing truly gets it clean—it's a constant worry for keeping the animals healthy. Then there's the drainage, which is a nightmare, and the ventilation system is archaic.' She ticked the items off on her fingers, each one a financial burden. 'They're all essential for the animals' well-being, every last one, but the costs are staggering. Our fundraising efforts, bless the hearts of those who've helped, haven't even scratched the surface."

"Can we see the dogs now?" Lyn interjected, desperate.

Martha brightened. "Of course! Grand tour? See where Sam spent his first weeks?"

We followed her through the door behind the counter, down

a hall lined with 'Happy Tail' photos. She pointed out the cat room ("Seven charming purr-machines"), a small vet clinic ("Dr. Patel volunteers twice a week, bless her"), and then, the barking growing louder, the main dog kennels.

The noise washed over us as she pushed open the door—barks, yips, and whines intensifying as the dogs sensed visitors. Twenty kennels lined the walls, about half occupied. The concrete floor, visibly worn despite cleaning, sloped toward central drains—the system needing replacement. The air hung thick with disinfectant battling underlying dogginess.

"Welcome to canine central," Martha announced over the din. "Eleven wonderful souls waiting for their second chance."

Lyn immediately darted to the nearest kennel, where a frantic spaniel mix pressed against the wire. Dad, however, scanned the overhead ventilation ducts critically. Mom moved slowly, reading info cards. I hesitated near the entrance, the wave of sound triggering a sharp memory—the noise when we first met Sam.

Martha noticed. "Something wrong, Will?"

"No, just..." I swallowed. "Where was Sam's kennel? Do you remember?"

She studied me a moment, then gestured toward the far end. "Last one on the right. Kennel twenty."

Drawn by an impulse I didn't examine, I walked that way, the barking seeming to recede as I focused. Kennel twenty housed a small black Lab puppy, Hank, asleep in a fluffy bed. I crouched down, looking into the space where Sam had waited. Worn concrete, hairline cracks like dry riverbeds. The chain-link gate bowed slightly outward.

The shelter memory washed over me with startling clarity. I was six, gripping Dad's hand tightly as we navigated this same cacophonous hallway. The smells had overwhelmed me—disinfectant, kibble, wet fur—until we'd stopped right here at kennel twenty. Inside, a white puppy with one flopped ear had sat perfectly still amid the chaos, watching us with those impossibly wise eyes. Not barking, not jumping—only observing with a calm intensity that seemed to say, "Finally. I've been waiting for you."

When the volunteer opened the gate, Sam walked directly to me, bypassing Dad, and placed one paw deliberately on my sneaker. "He's choosing you," Dad had said, his voice hushed with a sudden, unexpected wonder. Mom had leaned down and received a gentle nose bump against her cheek. Even Lyn, barely four and hiding behind Mom's legs, had giggled when Sam sat politely before her, waiting until she found the courage to touch his ear. We'd known instantly. Not just any dog. Our dog. Family.

This confining, bare space had been his world—until he became the heart of ours.

"Will! Over here! You have to see this one!" Lyn hissed urgently from a few kennels down.

Curious, I joined her. Inside sat a scruffy terrier mix with a tan and gray patchwork coat, nothing like Sam. But he sat alertly, head tilted at an angle so precise, so uncannily Sam, it sent a jolt through me. His dark, intelligent eyes held an unnerving focus.

"Look, Will," Lyn murmured. "The way he's sitting... just like Sam when he was listening hard."

As if understanding, the terrier's ears perked. His head tilted further.

"What's his story?" Dad asked, coming up behind us, Mom beside him.

Martha consulted the card. "That's Max. Been here about three months. Found wandering near the highway—no collar, no chip. Maybe two years old."

Max stood then, moving purposefully to the front. His dark, intelligent eyes found and locked onto mine, ignoring everyone else, carrying an intensity that felt less like simple curiosity and more like... recognition. A tremor ran through me.

"Can we...?" I began, unsure of the question myself.

"Meet him properly?" Martha offered readily. "Visitation room across the hall. Much nicer."

Lyn grabbed my arm, eyes shining. "Yes! Please?"

Martha looked over, fetching a slip lead. She entered the kennel calmly, speaking softly as she clipped the lead. Max remained composed, dark eyes never leaving my face.

"Follow me," Martha directed. "Marie, Albert, care to see the food prep area while the kids visit Max?"

Mom hesitated, glancing from Max to us.

"We're good, Mom," I assured her, needing this first encounter to be only Lyn and me.

"Visitation room's right there," Martha pointed. "Glass front."

Mom stood still for a moment. "Alright. We did want to discuss that donation."

Martha led Max into the visitation room—clean floor, plastic bench, basket of chewed toys. "Okay, get acquainted," she said, handing me the leash as she backed out. "Wave if you need anything. Showing your folks the administrative labyrinth—I mean, office."

The door clicked shut.

Max sat politely near the center, regarding us with that unnerving, intelligent focus.

"Okay, this is officially weird, right?" Lyn whispered, sinking cross-legged a few feet away. "Not just me?"

"Definitely not just you," I confirmed, joining her on the floor. "Something... familiar."

Max took a tentative step, then another, sniffing Lyn's outstretched hand, then mine. His tail gave a slow, hesitant wag.

"Hi, Max," Lyn murmured. "You seem like a really good boy.

Like our Sam was."

At the name 'Sam,' Max's ears flicked sharply. A low, almost mournful whine vibrated deep in his throat. He lifted his right paw and placed it deliberately, firmly, on my knee.

The exact gesture. Always the right paw. Sam's silent offering of comfort when words failed me. A crushing wave of memory hit me—the day before my first middle school dance, paralyzed with anxiety, Sam sitting beside me with that steady paw that somehow said, "I'm here. You'll be okay."

Lyn gasped beside me. "Will—did you—"

"I see it," I interrupted, my voice thick with emotion I couldn't contain. Coincidence crumbled away. With an unsteady hand, I reached to scratch behind Max's ears, finding the exact spot Sam loved—that little hollow just above the base. Max leaned into the touch, eyes half-closing, relaxing against my hand. Just like Sam.

"Do you think..." Lyn began, voice hushed with wonder. "Could he be... *reincarnated*?"

I shook my head slowly, reeling. "Pastor John thought Sam was still... Sam.
Somewhere else. Watching." I looked down at Max, who now turned to Lyn, offering his paw just as he had to me. Lyn took it gently, eyes suddenly glistening.

"He needs us, Will," she declared, emotion catching in her voice. "Look at him. He belongs with us."

The thought hit me with force, but practicality intruded. "Mom and Dad might say it's too soon. We just came to donate."

"But what if this is why we came?" Lyn insisted, conviction startling. "What if Sam *led* us here? The flower, the clouds— pointing to Max?"

The idea resonated, bypassing logic, feeling profoundly right. Could this scruffy terrier be the next step in Sam's guidance?

Just then, my eyes were drawn to the corner opposite the door. For a fraction of a second, the light seemed to waver there, shimmering like heat haze. Subtle, but Max reacted instantly. He withdrew his paw, his body tensing, his unwavering attention fixed like a beam on that corner, a low growl rumbling—not aggression, but acknowledgment.

The shimmer vanished. Max relaxed, shaking himself lightly, then looked back at us, head tilted inquisitively. Before we could process, the door opened. Mom peered in, Dad and Martha behind her.

"Everything alright?" Mom asked. "Thought we heard a growl."

Lyn and I exchanged a look. Later. "Fine," I answered, scratching Max again, my hand still unsteady. "He was just... checking out the toys."

Mom entered fully, taking in the scene—us on the floor, Max leaning companionably against my leg.

"Seems to have made himself right at home," Martha observed, stepping inside. "Quite something. Max is usually reserved with new people."

Dad crouched beside us, studying the terrier with new intensity. "Friendly little fella, isn't he?"

"He's perfect," Lyn burst out, seizing the moment. "Dad, Mom, we have to adopt him."

The plea hung in the air. Dad's eyebrows shot up, and his head turned towards Mom. I watched Mom's face; a complicated mix of emotions flickered there—a wince of fresh grief at the thought of another dog so soon, a shadow of empathy for Lyn's sudden, fierce hope, and then a careful, almost pained, settling of her features as she met Dad's questioning gaze.

"Lynnie," she began, her voice soft, each word seemingly chosen with immense care, "we only just lost Sam. Another dog so soon—"

"It's exactly the right moment!" Lyn countered, determination flashing in her eyes. "I'm convinced... Sam deliberately guided us to Max."

Her declaration, resonating with absolute conviction, carried unexpected impact.

Martha observed the exchange, her expression contemplative yet perceptive. "In my experience," she offered after a thoughtful pause, "these profound connections deserve our attention. Occasionally, they form instantly. When the match is genuine, everyone present recognizes the rightness."

Dad straightened, fingers raking through his hair—his unconscious gesture when confronting unanticipated situations. "Our intention was to make a donation," he reminded us, his tone authoritative yet not conclusive. "Adoption wasn't on today's agenda."

A brief silence settled, broken only by Max's soft panting. Mom's gaze drifted from Dad's set jaw to Lyn's hopeful face, then to Max, who seemed to watch her with an almost human understanding. An almost imperceptible sigh escaped her before she looked back at Dad, her expression clear and thoughtful.

"I wonder if we might consider both possibilities," Mom proposed gently, her support catching me off guard. "If... the connection proves authentic."

Another silent exchange between my parents.

"Let's... discuss it," Dad proposed finally, his tone shifting from resistant to considering. "Tonight. Sleep on it."

Martha approved. "Wise. Max isn't scheduled for events soon—honestly, not much interest these past months." She hesitated. "Though I should mention... with the budget... we might have to start making hard decisions soon. Possibly transferring longer-term residents to the county."

"The county facility?" Mom questioned, sensing the unspoken.

Martha's lips thinned. "Overcrowded. Under-resourced.

Strict time limits." The threat—Max's time potentially running out—felt palpable.

"What if we helped?" The words were out before I thought. "With the shelter?
Fundraising? Repairs?"

Martha looked startled. "Incredibly kind, Will, but the gap is significant. Around twenty thousand for mandated upgrades. We've barely raised a quarter."

"We're good at fundraising!" Lyn jumped in. "My soccer team got sponsors!"

Dad's expression shifted again, parental caution yielding to professional assessment. "What repairs are most critical?"

"Kennel flooring and drainage," Martha reiterated. "Sanitation risk. And ventilation."

Dad glanced toward the kennel hallway, mind visibly calculating. "That's... my line of work. Concrete, drainage, HVAC. Could take a look and give you an assessment. Maybe suggest cost-saving options."

Genuine hope sparked in Martha's tired eyes. "You'd do that? Albert, even a consultation... Contractors hear 'non-profit shelter' and run."

"I'll make time next week," Dad promised, decision made. "As for fundraising... kids seem motivated. And Marie," he glanced at Mom, "you rally the troops."

Mom showed a glinting determination. "The church

community. Pastor John mentioned supporting animal welfare."

A warmth spread through me. This felt right. Helping the place that gave us Sam, where we met this uncanny terrier... purpose clicking into place.

Martha beamed, clasping her hands. "I don't know what twist of fate brought you here," she said, voice thick with emotion, "but I'm starting to believe it was providence."

Lyn caught my eye. Providence, maybe. Or a very determined white dog looking out for his family.

Max, who had been observing peaceably, now stood and walked with that uncanny, purposeful air directly to Dad. With a solemn, thoughtful deliberation, he lifted his right paw and placed it firmly on Dad's knee.

Dad went rigid, his breath catching audibly. For a long moment, he just stared at the paw on his jeans as if it were a brand. Then, his own hand, large and work-roughened, moved with uncharacteristic hesitation before he finally reached down, his fingers gently ruffling the fur behind Max's ears.

A dry chuckle escaped him, the sound rusty from disuse. "Well," he murmured, his voice still holding a rough edge of disbelief, "you certainly know how to make an entrance."

Martha smiled knowingly. "Some dogs just connect. Max seems special—intuitive. Reminds me quite a bit of your Sam, that way."

As if on cue, Max turned, his dark eyes locking with unwavering intensity on that same corner where the light had shimmered. His tail gave two distinct, slow thumps against the floor. Nothing visible there, but his focused attention sent a clear message.

"I think," Mom said gently, "we should sleep on adoption, as Albert suggested. But we can leave the donation now."

Dad agreed, rising. "And I'll call Monday about that assessment."

"Thank you," Martha breathed, gratitude radiating. "More than you know."

As we prepared to leave, Lyn knelt for a final word with Max, whispering something that made his tail thump again. I joined her, giving him one last pat, a strange certainty settling over me that this wasn't goodbye. "We'll be back," I promised. Max tilted his head, intelligent eyes seeming to understand.

Just as Martha clipped the shelter lead back on, Max let out two sharp, distinct barks. Woof. Woof.

"That's funny," Martha remarked, pausing. "Exact signal we taught Sam for needing outside. Two quick barks, same rhythm. Never heard Max make that sound."

A shiver traced my spine. Confirmation. Beside me, Lyn's eyes widened, her hand finding mine, squeezing tightly.

Outside, buckling into the truck while Dad finalized the donation, Lyn leaned close. "Did you see it?" she whispered urgently. "The corner? The weird light?"

I hesitated. "Saw... something. A shimmer."

"It was Sam," she declared with absolute conviction. "And Max saw him too."

Before I could respond, Mom turned in the front seat. "You two really connected with Max. Are you sure you want us to seriously consider adopting"?

Lyn expressed approval emphatically. "Yes! One hundred percent! Please?"

I thought of Max's gestures, his focus, his response to Sam's name, and the double bark. The shimmer. "I think," I said deliberately, "we were meant to find him today. Maybe... maybe Sam led us here."

Dad slid into the driver's seat. He let out a low, conflicted sound—half scoff, half sigh—that noticeably lacked its usual sharp edge of skepticism. " Quite a leap, Will.

"But you can't deny he connected with all of us, Albert," Mom pointed out gently. "Especially the kids. And that bark..."

"Not denying anything," Dad replied, starting the engine, his tone surprisingly open. "Just saying it's a big decision. Needs thought."

As we pulled away, I twisted, looking back. Through the window, I saw Martha near the desk, Max sitting patiently beside her, head tilted questioningly. We turned onto Maple

Street, the shelter vanishing. But the image lingered, along with a growing certainty pulsing deep inside—our journey with Maple Street, and perhaps with Max, was far from over. It felt guided. Purposeful. Sam was still here, somehow. Not just memory, but actively shaping our path through uncanny terrors and pressing needs. The ache of absence began transforming—not gone, but filled now with unfolding purpose. As we drove, brainstorming fundraising ideas, Dad already outlining assessments, something vital stirred within me. Direction. Rightness. A sense that we were being led toward exactly where we needed to be.

Dinner that evening carried an undercurrent of excitement despite Dad's insistence on "sleeping on" the adoption decision. Mom prepared lasagna—comfort food that filled the kitchen with familiar, grounding aromas. The empty space beneath the table, where Sam would normally lie hoping for dropped morsels, felt less achingly vacant than it had for weeks.

"So he just... knew the command for outside?" Lyn asked, serving herself a second helping of garlic bread. "Without anyone teaching him?"

"That's what Martha said," I confirmed, sneaking a tiny piece of cheese to Max, who sat attentively beside my chair, mastering the art of polite begging with remarkable speed. "Same bark pattern Sam used."

"Coincidence, maybe," Dad suggested, though his skepticism lacked its usual edge. "Dogs have limited vocalization patterns."

"Two identical barks, same pitch, same timing?" Mom

countered gently. She passed the salad bowl in his direction. "That's quite specific, Albert."

Dad accepted the bowl, his expression thoughtful rather than dismissive. Progress. "He does seem unusually... attuned," he acknowledged, glancing down at Max, who returned his look with that unnerving intelligence. "Martha mentioned he hadn't connected with other potential adopters?"

"Three months at the shelter," I confirmed. "Multiple meet-and-greets, but no connection."

"Until us," Lyn added pointedly. "Specifically us. Sam's family."

A comfortable silence settled over the table as we each processed this. The coincidences were stacking up beyond statistical probability—the flower, the clouds, and now this remarkably familiar dog appearing exactly when the shelter faced its greatest crisis.

"He'd need proper training," Dad said finally, setting down his fork. "Regular walks. Veterinary visits aren't cheap."

Mom's eyes met mine across the table, a flicker of hope passing between us. Dad was considering logistics, not objecting on principle.

"I'll walk him before school," Lyn volunteered immediately. "And on weekends."

"We could split the responsibilities," I added. "I can handle afternoon walks; make sure he's exercised."

Max's tail thumped against the floor, as if he understood the conversation's direction. Perhaps he did.

"We'd need supplies," Dad continued, his tone shifting further toward planning rather than hypothesizing. "Bed, food, proper leash."

"Martha said we could use the shelter's starter kit for adopted dogs," Mom reminded him. "And Dr. Patel offers discount checkups for shelter adoptions."

Dad stood, absorbing this information. His eyes rested on Max, studying him thoughtfully, who met Dad's scrutiny with a steady, knowing regard.

"We'll visit again tomorrow," he decided finally. "See if this... connection... holds up. If it does..." He left the sentence unfinished, but his unspoken meaning hung in the air, as palpable as if he'd shouted it.

Under the table, Max inched slightly closer to my chair, leaning warmly against my leg. The pressure, the specific way he settled, was an echo of Sam, so instantly recognized that it both ached and healed simultaneously. Not replacing Sam, but continuing something vital. Building upon foundations already established.

CHAPTER 6:
FIRST STEPS FORWARD

Sunday morning dawned bright, the air outside clear and carrying the scent of damp earth washed clean by yesterday's storm. I lay watching sunlight slant through the blinds, dust motes dancing like miniature galaxies. The memory of Maple Street echoed—Max's uncanny echoes of Sam, Dad's unexpected offer to help, and the undercurrent of purpose that had settled over us on the drive home.

Downstairs, the well-worn rhythm of Mom preparing for church—cabinets opening, water running—felt different today, overlaid with a hum of anticipation. Usually, I'd groan and burrow deeper under the covers, dreading stiff clothes and long sermons. Today, I actually wanted to go. Pastor John would be there. After yesterday, I needed to understand more.

I swung my legs over the side of the bed. The house felt... lighter. The weight of grief hadn't vanished, but it had shifted, becoming something carried together, not shouldered alone.

Jeans, a reasonably unwrinkled shirt. The bathroom door was locked. Predictable.

"Lyn," I called, knocking twice. "Need the bathroom."

"Be right there!" she sang out, sounding ridiculously cheerful. Last Sunday, this scenario had ended in a shouting match.

The door opened, releasing a cloud of floral steam. Lyn emerged in a blue dress I hadn't seen before, hair pulled back neatly.

"You look... dressy," I observed.

She shrugged, a smile playing on her lips. "Pastor John might want to talk about the shelter. And Max."

"Still set on him?" I asked, though her conviction yesterday had been absolute.

"Aren't you?" She gave me a knowing look. "You *saw* him. You *felt* it." Before I could respond, she sailed past toward the stairs. I shook my head. Since when did my impulsive sister possess such certainty about unseen things? Grief, maybe. Or maybe she was just listening better than I was.

Splashing cold water on my face, I met my reflection. More rested than I'd felt in days.

Sadness still shadowed my eyes, but it was tempered now with something else—purpose. An unexpected gift from a scruffy terrier mix and a struggling shelter.

Downstairs, Mom flipped pancakes, already dressed for church. Dad sat reading the paper—not sports, but an article on community grants—a tie loosely knotted over his button-down. Even he seemed different.

"Morning, Will," Mom greeted, sliding a plate onto the table. "Sleep okay?"

"Yeah. Actually." I slid into my chair, surprised by hunger. "Smells great."

Dad lowered his paper, looking over reading glasses that gave him an unusual scholarly air. "Your mother and I were talking. About yesterday."

My stomach tightened. "Max?"

"Everything," Mom clarified, joining us. "The shelter, the fundraising, Dad's assessment idea... and Max."

"And?" Lyn prompted, arriving with perfect timing.

Dad and Mom exchanged one of their silent glances. "We think helping the shelter is the right thing to do," Dad began deliberately. "I called Martha this morning and scheduled the assessment for Tuesday."

"And," Mom continued, "we'll talk to Pastor John after service about involving the church. Maybe directing summer festival proceeds?"

Hope swelled, but Lyn cut to the chase. "What about Max?"

Another glance between them. "We think," Dad said slowly, "we should visit him again. Together. See if yesterday's connection holds."

"If it does," Mom added, her eyes finding mine, a silent promise of understanding passing between us, "we'll start the adoption process."

Lyn let out a squeal, launching herself at Dad in a hug. "Thank you!"

He looked startled but pleased, patting her back awkwardly. "Hold on, Lynnie. Need to be sure it's right for everyone—including him."

"It is," Lyn declared with unwavering conviction. "You'll see."

Mom watched me. "What do you think, Will?"

The question deserved honesty. Amidst the excitement, a flicker of hesitation remained—adopting Max felt like acknowledging Sam was truly gone, even while honoring his memory. "I think," I began slowly, "Max needs us. And maybe... maybe we need him. Not replacing Sam. Something new."

Mom's expression softened. "That's a good way to put it."

Dad folded his paper decisively. "Settled then. Visit tomorrow after school."

"And now," Mom added, glancing at the clock, "finish breakfast, or we'll be late."

Twenty minutes later, all four of us piled into Dad's truck—a Sunday rarity, as he usually found work excuses. Today he drove, a low, almost tuneless whistle drifting from his lips, the tension that had gripped him yesterday noticeably replaced by a quiet resolve.

First Community Church sat white and sturdy under the morning sun, steeple pointing skyward. The parking lot buzzed with familiar cars.

"Will," Mom said as we unbuckled, "Pastor John wants to speak with you after. Okay?"

I paced the area, anxiety fluttering despite wanting the conversation. What would he ask?

The sanctuary welcomed us with organ music and murmured greetings. Sunlight streamed through stained glass, painting colors across the pews. We slid into our usual spot. Mrs. Chen turned, smiling. "Marie! Albert! Wonderful to see you all." Her eyebrows lifted slightly seeing Dad. "Children look well."

Molly appeared beside her mother, offering a tentative smile my way. "Hi, Will. Feeling better?"

"Yeah, thanks," I answered, touched by her concern. School felt distant.

"Heard about your dog," she said softly as our parents chatted. "Really sorry."

"Thanks." What else could I say? How to explain clouds, flowers, and uncanny terriers?

Molly seemed to sense the impossibility. "Well, if you need anything..."

"Appreciate it," I told her, meaning it.

The organ swelled. Pastor John appeared at the pulpit, his warm, appraising eyes sweeping over the congregation, lingering briefly on our family, a subtle nod acknowledging Dad's presence.

The service began—hymns, readings, and announcements. I drifted, thoughts returning to Max, to tomorrow's visit. Would he still feel familiar? Would that corner shimmer again?

Pastor John's sermon topic jolted me back. "Today," he began, his voice calm and resonant, "I'd like to talk about signs and wonders."

Beside me, Lyn straightened. Mom's hand found Dad's. Not a coincidence, I thought.

"Throughout scripture," Pastor John continued, "God communicates in unexpected ways—burning bushes, dreams, even animals." His look broadened, taking in every face in the sanctuary. "These messages often appear in times of grief or uncertainty, guiding us toward purpose when we feel most lost."

The sermon unfolded, feeling directed yet universal. He spoke of openness to guidance, finding meaning in service, and the healing power of community. He never looked directly at us again, but the message felt tailored and affirming.

As the final hymn began, Mom leaned close. "Pastor John asked if you could meet him in his office after."

I acknowledged my surroundings again, nerves tightening.

The benediction finally came. As people filed out, Mom guided me toward a side door marked "Church Offices." "We'll wait in the fellowship hall. Take your time."

The hallway smelled of coffee and old paper. I followed shuffling sounds to an open door. Pastor John sat behind a cluttered desk—notebooks, mugs, and a half-built model airplane. He looked up, smiling. "William, come in. Thanks for making time."

"Sure." I stepped inside. The office felt surprisingly comfortable—overflowing bookshelves, children's art, and a worn leather couch.

"Have a seat," he invited, gesturing to a chair. "Won't keep you long."

I sank into the chair. "Your sermon..."

"Yes?" he prompted gently.

"It felt... specific. About Sam?"

He regarded me levelly. "Recent events certainly informed my thoughts. But the message applies broadly—we all need reminders to stay open to guidance." He leaned forward. "William, I asked to speak with you because I sense you have questions perhaps difficult to ask in front of your family."

His perception disarmed me. "I don't know what to believe," I admitted. "About Sam, what we're seeing. It feels real, but my mind..."

"Struggles to reconcile it," Pastor John finished calmly. "Entirely natural. Especially for an analytical mind like yours."

"Ms. Winters talks to you?"

He chuckled. "Eleanor and I are on the school board. She's mentioned your untapped potential."

His expression grew serious. "But I meant your tendency to observe, question, and seek evidence. Valuable traits, William, not obstacles to faith."

The knot of confusion began to unravel. "So I shouldn't just... accept it without question?"

"Certainly not," he replied, sounding surprised. "Faith and intellect aren't opposed; they inform each other. The greatest theologians were profound thinkers." He rose and retrieved a worn leather book from a shelf. "You know those classic children's stories? Magical world, talking animals, a great lion?"

"I read the first one in fifth grade," I said with confidence, recognizing the unspoken reference.

"The author," Pastor John continued, placing the book on the desk, "was a renowned intellectual who came to faith through reason, not by abandoning it." The book's title: *Finding Faith Through Reason*. "This might interest you later. My point is, your questions are part of how you process these experiences."

It felt like permission. "Sometimes I think I see Sam," I

confessed, the words rushing out. "Not just clouds or flowers, but... glimpses. Like he's still here. Yesterday, at the shelter, with Max—the corner seemed to shimmer? Max reacted, like he saw something too."

Pastor John said slowly, with no hint of dismissal. "I believe you, William. And I believe these experiences are meaningful, whether literal manifestations or divine guidance taking a form you'll recognize."

"But how do I know which?" I pressed, needing certainty.

He smiled gently. "That's where faith enters. We don't always get certainty. We observe, consider, pray... and move forward understanding complete knowledge isn't always granted."

Frustration surfaced. "Not very helpful."

He laughed warmly. "No, perhaps not in the way you mean. But consider: does it ultimately matter if you're seeing Sam's spirit or experiencing God's guidance through Sam's memory? The effect is the same—you're being led toward something meaningful."

I thought about it. "The shelter. Helping save it."

"And perhaps more," Pastor John suggested. "Your family is coming together. Healing is happening. Connections forming. Profound outcomes, regardless of the precise cause."

He was right. Dad at church. Mom humming again. Lyn and I actually talking.

Something was shifting.

"Think we're going to adopt Max," I told him, the decision solidifying as I spoke it. "The dog from the shelter. He feels... connected."

No surprise showed on Pastor John's face. "Martha Wilson called this morning. Mentioned your visit, the remarkable bond with Max." He smiled slightly. "Martha isn't prone to exaggeration. When she described it as 'meant to be,' I paid attention."

I asked Pastor John if he knew Martha well.

"Her late husband Edward was a church elder for years. Martha's devoted her life to caring for God's creatures—a ministry in its own right." He leaned back. "The shelter's troubles have concerned me. I'm glad your family feels called to help."

A thought surfaced. "At the shelter, Max looked at that corner like he saw something. And sometimes sunlight hits him, and he looks almost... white. Like Sam." I hesitated. "Could Sam be... working through Max?"

Pastor John regarded me intently. "History holds accounts of animals sharing profound spiritual bonds, unexplained knowledge transfer. I wouldn't dismiss it." He rose, moving to the window.

"What I know is this: love doesn't end. The bonds continue, though their nature changes. Whether Sam's spirit guides you directly or his memory shapes events, the love remains constant. That's the truth at faith's heart, William—love endures."

His words resonated—continuity, connection despite separation. Not replacement, but transformation. "Think I understand," I said slowly. "Partly."

He turned from the window, expression warm. "That's all any of us can claim. The rest is faith." He glanced at his watch. "I should let you go. My door is always open."

Rising, I felt unburdened. "Thank you, Pastor John."

He walked me to the door. "One more thing, William. Your experiences—these are personal gifts. You don't owe explanations to those who don't understand. Some things are held in the heart." He paused. "That said," with a knowing look, "your father's journey here is important. His skepticism isn't rejection; it's his way of processing something that challenges his worldview. Be patient."

"I'll try."

In the fellowship hall, my family gathered with coffee and donuts. Dad deep in conversation with Mr. Jenkins about roofing. Mom and Lyn chatting with Mrs. Peterson.

Ordinary Sunday morning scene. Yet nothing felt ordinary anymore.

"There he is," Mom said, spotting me. "Everything okay?"

"Yeah," I answered, surprised to find it true. "Everything's good."

Chapter 7:

Guiding Light

Red digits glowed 6:15 AM. My eyes flew open, heart hammering against my ribs—not from the alarm, but from the sheer, vibrant intensity of the dream still clinging to me. Sam. He'd been running, a joyful white streak through an endless field of flowers, each bloom a perfect, luminous echo of the one that defied season beneath our oak. Then he'd stopped, turning to fix me with that soulful, knowing gaze before letting out two sharp, urgent barks. The meaning hovered just out of reach, a message shrouded in mist, yet a certainty resonated in my chest: it was profoundly important. Could dreams, I wondered, truly be pathways?

A low, insistent whine drifted up from downstairs. Max. I swung my legs out of bed, fingers brushing against the disposable camera I'd bought yesterday, now sitting on my nightstand. Twenty-three exposures left. Dad had raised an eyebrow but hadn't pressed when I'd mumbled something about a science project. I hadn't told anyone I planned to document the sky, needing some kind of proof, a tangible anchor for these glimpses of a world that wasn't supposed to exist.

Through the window, dawn painted ribbons of high cirrus clouds across a deepening blue. Light caught their edges, turning them gold. For a second, the arrangement shifted— was that a suggestion of movement? Floppy ears? Hope surged. I grabbed the camera, framed the shot—but the breeze sighed, feathers of vapor shifted, dissolved.

Gone. Or perhaps never truly there. My breath hitched. *Was I chasing ghosts?*

Max whined again, more insistent. Lyn's door stayed shut. Figures. I pulled a sweatshirt over pajamas, camera clutched tight, and padded downstairs.

Mom stood at the back door, bathrobe belted loosely, holding it open as Max darted into the yard. Morning light slanted long across the dew-kissed grass. He raced to the fence, paused to investigate intently, then resumed his perimeter patrol.

"Sorry if he woke you," Mom said, stifling a yawn. "Still adjusting."

"Already awake," I told her. "Dreamed about Sam."

A gentle light came into Mom's eyes, and the tight lines of worry around her mouth seemed to ease. Her expression lightened up. "A good one?"

I think so. Running through flowers—like *that* one." I looked toward the oak, where the single white blossom still stood, luminous and perfect, as if untouched by time or weather. "Felt like he was trying to tell me something.

Mom tilted her head, her gaze turning inward for a moment as if she were sifting through her own quiet beliefs. "Maybe dreams are how they reach us easiest," she said, her voice imbued with a soft certainty that resonated with my own budding hope. "Minds quieter then." Her acceptance, spoken with such gentle conviction, felt like a small miracle itself.

"Thought I saw something in the clouds just now, too," I admitted, gesturing with the camera. "Changed before I could snap it."

"You'll get it," Mom assured me. "He'll make sure."

We observed Max crisscrossing the lawn, his trajectory unerringly drawing him toward the oak. As he approached Sam's grave, his exuberant movement transformed abruptly.

His pace became measured, deliberate. Upon reaching the white flower, he assumed a poised sitting position, head angled upward—attention focused not on the tree itself, but on the seemingly vacant space beside it. Ears alert. Attentive.

"Watch," I whispered. "It's happening again."

We remained motionless, observing intently. Almost sixty seconds elapsed. Then, as though acknowledging unheard instructions, Max delivered two barks—crisp, purposeful, precisely matching the rhythm from my dream—before returning toward the house at an unhurried pace.

The hair on my forearms stood on end. "You witnessed that?"

"I did," Mom confirmed. "He wasn't just looking at the flower." The unspoken hung between us: Max wasn't alone out there.

Just as I raised the camera, hoping to capture some lingering trace, the morning atmosphere changed. The air between the kitchen window and the oak tree seemed to densify, creating a distortion like heat rising from summer pavement. It centered on the oak, the flower, and the empty space where Max had fixed his attention. Except—for a stunning, heart-stopping instant—it wasn't empty. Within that shimmering air materialized a familiar silhouette: white, four-legged, one ear characteristically flopped.

Unmistakably Sam. Substantial, yet see-through. Present.

I fumbled, pressing the shutter, knowing even as the plastic clicked that film couldn't capture this. Some things existed beyond lenses and chemicals. The silhouette dispersed as quickly as it had formed.

"You saw him too?" Mom asked, her voice so low it was almost carried away by the breeze, her eyes wide and fixed on the spot where the apparition had been.

I could only nod, throat tight. Seeing signs was one thing. Seeing him...
Mom let Max in. He entered deliberately, his keen eyes flicking from Mom's face to mine and back again, as if gauging our understanding. When Mom knelt, he licked her hand once, then padded over, pressing his side firmly against my legs. Sam's exact pressure.

Comfort offered, received.

"I think," Mom said, her voice still hushed with the wonder

of the sighting, a profound, almost peaceful certainty settling in her eyes as she watched Max and me, "Sam sent him. Not a replacement. A companion. A continuation."

The idea resonated, clarifying feelings I couldn't name. Max wasn't instead of Sam; he was because of Sam. Connected. Guided. Carrying a purpose.

"The shelter meeting tonight," I said suddenly, the dream's urgency clicking into place. "That's what Sam meant. It's important. More than we realize."

Mom considered this, expression serious. "You think Sam is... involved? In saving the shelter?"

"I think he's been guiding us all along," I replied, certainty solidifying. "The clouds, the flower, leading us to Max, the shelter needing help right when we reconnect... it all fits. It's his purpose for us."

The understanding felt immense—not a burden, but a direction. We weren't just fundraising; we were fulfilling a mission orchestrated by a love that bridged worlds.

"Well," Mom said, her practical side surfacing, "then we better make sure tonight's meeting is a success."

The morning unfolded with new focus. While Mom made breakfast, I filled Max's bowl, then sketched fundraiser poster ideas at the table. The cloud photography project felt different now—less science, more a chronicle of Sam's enduring connection and the ways he still touched our lives.

Dad came downstairs, dressed for errands, pausing in

surprise. "Up early."

"Couldn't sleep." I didn't elaborate.

He poured coffee, peered over my shoulder at the sketches. "Look good. Posters for tonight?"

"For the whole fundraiser. Put them around town."

Dad nodded approvingly. "Smart. Visuals help." He hesitated. "How's that science fair project coming? Cloud study?"

His interest surprised me. "It's good. Documenting formations. Identifying patterns."

"Any particular patterns?" His tone was casual, but his eyes held focused curiosity.

I chose words carefully. "Shapes that repeat. Formations that seem... meaningful."

Dad sipped his coffee, his eyes unfocusing as they drifted toward the window, toward the oak, lingering there for a long moment before he turned back to me. "Your mother mentioned... clouds reminding you of Sam."

My pulse quickened. I braced for the usual dismissal. But his voice, when he continued, was different—lower, edged with a reluctance I hadn't heard before. Confidential.

"Witnessed something yesterday myself," he began, then stopped, running a hand over his face as if to clear away lingering disbelief. "Driving back from Millfield. There was this... this cloud formation over the highway. So distinct, Will, that several cars actually pulled onto the shoulder to look." He paused, and his voice dropped to barely a murmur, his eyes unfocused as if replaying the image. "A perfect silhouette of a dog running. Alongside a smaller one. Like a freeze-frame. Lasted maybe thirty seconds."

The implication hung in the charged air between us. He wasn't just acknowledging my experience; he'd had his own. "Were you able to photograph it?" I asked, my own voice hushed.

He shook his head, a slow, almost rueful movement. "No camera on hand. But I've replayed it in my mind a hundred times." His gaze, when it finally met mine, was raw, stripped of its usual defenses. He leaned forward slightly, forearms on the table, his voice dropping even further, a tremor of something like awe—or perhaps fear—lacing its usual gruffness. "I can't rationalize all this, Will. The clouds, that flower.

His admission—his uncertainty, his willingness to consider—felt huge. I took a chance.

"I think Sam's still with us," I said plainly. "Watching. Showing us the next step."

Dad didn't argue. He looked thoughtful. "The shelter project?"

"Part of it. Helping save the place that gave him to us."

"Full circle," Dad murmured. Then, shaking his head briefly, as if dispelling overwhelming thoughts, he returned to practicalities. "Should get going. Pick up supplies for tonight. Want to ride along? Use a hand."

The invitation felt like another shift. "Sure. Let me get dressed."

Loading folding chairs from the church into his truck an hour later, Dad's cloud sighting echoed in my mind. Two dogs running. Sam and Max?

The town hummed with Saturday activity. Everything looked normal, yet my perception felt altered, tuned to possibilities beyond the visible.

"Stop at the print shop," Dad announced. "Fundraiser flyers should be ready."

Inside the narrow shop, the scent of ink and paper filled the air. Mr. Patterson peered through thick glasses. "Albert Thomas! Right on time." He retrieved a glossy stack. "Turned out well, I think."

Dad examined one, eyebrows rising. "Excellent, Henry. Better than expected."

Curiosity drew me closer. My breath caught. The flyer background: a stylized cloudy sky. Foreground: silhouettes of two dogs—one larger, one tinier—against a setting sun. Bold text: "SAVE MAPLE STREET ANIMAL SHELTER."

"Dad," I managed, the link between the flyer's image and his recent cloud sighting striking me with the force of a revelation. "This design..."

He looked over slightly in my direction, acknowledging my unspoken question. "Henry created it. Said the idea just... came to him."

Mr. Patterson beamed, oblivious. "Something about your description sparked it. Big dog watching over the little one— shelter's protective role, see?"

Or someone watching over all of us, I thought.

"How much?" Dad asked, reaching for his wallet.

Mr. Patterson waved it away. "My contribution. Daughter adopted her beagle there ten years ago. Best dog ever." Another connection.

Carrying the flyers, I studied the image. The larger silhouette held subtle echoes of Sam—lop-sided ears, tail curve. Too specific for mere chance.

"Did you give Mr. Patterson photos?" I asked Dad as we climbed into the truck.

He shook his head, starting the engine, brow slightly furrowed. "No. Just explained the fundraiser." After a pause, he added, "Some things... don't have neat explanations, Will."

His phone chirped. Mom. Extra tables needed from Pastor John's office.

The church stood still. Pastor John met us. "Tables are back here," he explained, leading us down the hall. "Albert, three more families committed to helping. Word's spreading."

Dad stepped in. "Good. Need all hands."

As they discussed logistics, my attention drifted, snagging on a bulletin board covered with children's drawings of heaven. One stood out—blue sky, cloud-animals looking down. Caption: "Where pets go."

"Interesting perspective," Pastor John observed, noticing my focus. "Children often grasp spiritual truths intuitively."

I thought of my cloud sightings. "Do you think it's possible? Animals... continuing?"

He considered this. "Many traditions believe in animal spiritual essence. Specifics vary, but the core idea persists—love continues beyond physical form." His careful answer validated without confining.

"I've been seeing things," I admitted while Dad wrestled with tables. "Clouds, dreams, glimpses... of Sam. Like he's still watching."

Pastor John met my eyes. "Have these continued?"

"This morning," I confirmed. "The dream. Then near his grave. Max saw something too."

"Animals often sense what we can't," he observed. "Perception isn't limited by skepticism."

"Do you think Sam is influencing us?" I asked. "Is there a purpose?"

His expression grew contemplative. "Purpose often reveals

itself through action, William. Following nudges of compassion, love—regardless of source—frequently shows us why we were nudged." He paused. "Whether Sam's influence is literal or metaphorical may matter less than your family's response—coming together."

His words resonated. The how mattered less than the why.

Dad returned. Pastor John handed me a leather-bound book. "Might find this interesting," he said. "Explores different perspectives on the spiritual nature of animals." The cover read: Faithful Companions: Spiritual Bonds Between Humans and Animals. "Keep it."

I thanked him, tucking it away. Another piece of the puzzle.

Back home, preparations for the evening meeting accelerated. Mom and Lyn arranged the living room; Dad and I set up chairs. Max shadowed us, occasionally freezing to stare at empty corners, head tilted.

During a lull, I retreated with Pastor John's book, reading accounts of animals as messengers, guides, continuing influences. One passage leaped out: "...a beloved animal that has passed may continue to watch over... sometimes manifesting... through another animal that serves as a conduit."

Max as a conduit. The idea clicked, explaining his uncanny behaviors, his immediate bond, his sensitivity.

A light knock. Mom peered in. "Will? Molly Chen's on the phone. Library meeting?"

The library! I'd forgotten. 1:30 already; meeting at 2:00. "Tell her I'm on my way," I said, closing the book, grabbing my cloud notebook. "Just running late."

Mom raised an eyebrow. "Library? Saturday?"

"Science fair research," I offered vaguely.

"Alright. Back by five—need setup help." She hesitated. "Take your camera. Sky looks interesting."

She was right. Dramatic cloud towers built in the west. Perfect.

The ride took me past the oak. Max sat beside the white flower, posture attentive, gaze fixed on empty air beside the tree. He remained utterly still for nearly a minute, then barked twice—that distinct pattern—rose, and trotted toward the house. Before biking on, I raised my camera, snapping one photo of the scene—tree, flower, the space Max had focused on. Something told me this image might hold more than met the eye.

Molly waited on the library steps, notebook and camera ready. She waved warmly.

"Sorry I'm late," I apologized, locking my bike. "Fundraiser stuff."

"No problem. Reading." She held up a meteorology text. "Reference for our cloud project."

Our cloud project. The words felt significant. "Brought my observation notebook. New photos."

Inside, at a quaint table, I described the morning clouds scientifically.

"Cirrocumulus patterns interesting for shape recognition," Molly noted, showing her own photos. "Brain seeks patterns—pareidolia."

"Think that's all it is?" I asked. "Our brains?"

She considered. "Pattern recognition is evolutionary. Doesn't mean patterns aren't meaningful." She paused. "Meaning can come from interpretation, not just neurological default." Her perspective—scientific yet open—echoed Pastor John's.

"I saw something this morning," I admitted. "A cloud like Sam. Gone before I could photograph it, but it was him."

I braced for skepticism. She just stared. "You mentioned seeing him before. Other times?"

The question opened the door. I found myself sharing more—the flower's growth, the collar sounds, the morning glimpse by the grave. I stopped short of calling Max a conduit.

When I finished, Molly turned a pencil slowly, her brow furrowed not with skepticism, but with deep thought.

"That's... extraordinary," she said finally, her voice quiet.

"Most would dismiss it. But multiple family members all experiencing aspects of it..."

She shook her head slightly, a small smile playing on her lips. "My own grandmother, who helped start the Maple Street shelter with her husband, used to tell the most amazing stories about some of the animals there—things they knew, people they helped in ways no one could explain. We always just thought they were sweet family tales, but..."

She looked at me then, her expression clear and direct.

"Don't think I'm crazy?"

"My perspective, Will," she articulated precisely, "is that scientific understanding of consciousness and the way consciousness itself might link to other consciousness remains incomplete. Perhaps love functions beyond current physical models."

She paused thoughtfully. "According to my grandfather, love represents the singular force that continually eludes scientific quantification. That principle might extend to animal-human bonds as well." Her assessment resonated profoundly, as if another piece of a complex puzzle had just clicked into place in my mind.

"Consider this possibility," Molly continued, her expression animated with scholarly enthusiasm, "we could expand our project's parameters. Beyond mere clouds, incorporating multiple variables—temporal patterns, emotional states, geographic factors, Max's behavioral responses?"

This reformulation transformed the project's entire dimension—evolving from basic pattern recognition toward methodical documentation of unexplained phenomena, presented within scientific frameworks. Ingenious. "Brilliant approach," I agreed, intellectual excitement mounting. "A comprehensive matrix of interrelated variables. Systematically tracking manifestations across contexts."

"Precisely!" Molly reciprocated my enthusiasm. "Applying stringent documentation protocols to observed phenomena, identifying potential correlations, while acknowledging interpretive frameworks that transcend strict materialism."

We spent the next hour developing a framework, lost in the work, ideas flowing easily between us.

"Should head back," I said finally, checking the time. "Promised Mom help."

"Meeting's at your house?" Molly asked, gathering materials. "Dad mentioned wanting to attend. Thinks the chem department might donate old equipment for the shelter's vet office." Another connection. Serendipity felt less random now, more like guided arrangement.

"Great. More support helps."

Stepping outside, the air itself felt different—charged, as if the earlier humidity had been scoured away, leaving a crystalline clarity. Above, the scattered cloud towers they'd noted earlier were gone. In their place, stark white against the deep azure, a new shape resolved itself. Not Sam this time. William's breath caught as his eyes traced the unlikely, sharp edges of an open book—edges far too defined for mere vapor—its pages seemingly frozen mid-turn by an unseen celestial hand.

"Look, Molly," I pointed. "Another formation."

Molly, who had been adjusting her camera settings, looked up. Her hands, usually so quick and precise with her equipment, stilled completely. Her lips parted slightly, and for a long moment, the usual analytical spark in her eyes was eclipsed by something softer, a reflection of pure, unadulterated wonder. Then, as if remembering herself, she blinked and swiftly raised her own camera.

"Remarkable stability," she murmured, more to herself than to me, before she began capturing several images as the clouds remained fixed, unnaturally stable, as if ensuring we recognized their meaning before dispersing.

A book. Knowledge. Stories unfolding. New chapters. The symbolism resonated—Pastor John's book, our research project, the shelter's next phase. Sam's guidance, demonstrating not just presence, but purpose.

"Message received," I whispered skyward. "We're understanding."

The journey home felt transformed, infused with direction. The distinct feeling of Sam's spirit accompanied us— unseen but undeniable, a nurturing force surrounding us.

CHAPTER 8:

BENEATH THE SURFACE

A strange hum persisted beneath my skin, a low-frequency buzz that had started after visiting Maple Street and intensified over the past two days. It wasn't just Max, though the terrier's uncanny echoes of Sam were a constant thrum in my thoughts as he adjusted to our home. This felt different. A pull. An insistent nudge toward unfinished business.

Dad wasn't scheduled to assess the shelter until Tuesday, but waiting felt increasingly wrong, like ignoring a persistent tapping on the windowpane. By Saturday afternoon, the feeling was undeniable—a magnetic draw eastward, toward the shelter.

"Mom," I ventured after lunch, aiming for casual, "thinking I might bike over to the shelter? See if Martha needs help?"

Mom lowered her book, her gaze settling on me, perceptive, lingering. I braced for questions I couldn't quite answer. "That's thoughtful, Will," she said finally, her voice even, betraying nothing. "Are you sure?"

"Yeah, just... feel like I should." I shrugged, the excuse feeling paper-thin even to me.

"What about Max?" she asked, glancing toward the living room where he'd curled up after his morning walk.

"I'll take him," I decided, sensing somehow that he should be part of this. "He might like visiting his old friends."

A flicker of understanding—or maybe just intuition—crossed her face. "Alright. Be back by dinner. Take your phone."

Relief hit like a cool wave. Max perked up immediately when I grabbed his leash, as if he'd been waiting for this invitation. The bike ride felt charged, the familiar country road crackling with an unseen energy. I pedaled slowly, Max trotting alongside on his leash, both of us feeling less like we were deciding to go and more like we were being sent.

Martha waved distractedly from her cluttered office when we arrived, phone pressed to her ear, deep in what sounded like damage control with a disgruntled donor. "Take him out back!" she called, turning away, barely registering that it was Max returning for a visit.

But Max had other ideas. He planted his feet, claws digging subtly into the worn linoleum. He pulled firmly, insistently, toward the kennel corridor, toward the clatter and echo of the dogs.

"Not that way, Max," I attempted, tugging gently. "It's noisy back there."

He dismissed my guidance completely, head lowered, muscles tense, pulling with quiet but unwavering resolve. This wasn't a dog seeking exercise. This was a dog executing a mission. A chill ran up my spine. Okay, Sam, I thought, *what* are you revealing to us?

I released tension on the leash. Max took command.

The familiar barking cacophony engulfed us, but Max navigated through the uproar as though insulated by singular purpose, his focus unwavering. He passed the excitable spaniel without a glance, ignored the howling beagle, proceeding directly toward the far end—kennel twenty.

Hank, the Lab puppy, tumbled with a toy, oblivious. Max paid him no mind. His attention locked onto the concrete floor near the back wall. He began sniffing intently, nose hovering inches above the ground, a low tremor running through his body. He circled the spot twice, a tight, focused rotation, then sat directly over the dark metal drainage grate near the corner. He stared down at it, head cocked, listening, deciphering something beyond my perception.

"What is it, boy?" I whispered, crouching beside him. The kennel noise faded to a background roar as my focus narrowed. "Just the drain."

But looking closer, it wasn't quite right. The grate didn't sit perfectly flush; one edge lifted maybe a hair's breadth, catching a slight shadow. The metal looked older, more pitted than others along the aisle. As I leaned in, tracing the uneven edge, the fluorescent tube overhead flickered harshly, sputtering before stabilizing, casting strange, dancing shadows around that specific spot. Simultaneously, a pocket of intense cold brushed my skin, localized right there, raising goosebumps despite the stuffy air.

Max whined again, higher pitched, and pointedly nudged the raised edge of the grate with his nose. He looked up at me, dark eyes holding an expression of urgent, intelligent expectation.

My heart began a frantic, heavy thrum against my breastbone. This wasn't random. Max's insistence, the flickering light, the sudden pocket of intense cold... every nerve ending I possessed screamed that this was orchestrated. Guided.

Kneeling fully, the cool dampness of the concrete seeping into my jeans, a tremor of anticipation—or was it fear?— shot through my arms as I hooked my fingers under the grate's edge. Heavy cast iron. It resisted for a moment, then shifted with a reluctant groan. Gritting my teeth, I pulled harder. With a loud, scraping screech of metal on concrete, the grate tilted back against the kennel wall.

The opening wasn't just shallow pipe access. It was deeper—a small, rough rectangle hollowed in the sub-flooring, its depths choked with dust, cobwebs, and desiccated leaves that whispered of long-forgotten years. And nestled there, half-buried in decades of grime, lay a dull grey metal box. My breath hitched. Time seemed to slow, the distant barking of the other dogs fading to a dull roar as all my focus narrowed onto that one, impossible object.

Ancient-looking, like salvaged treasure, though probably just old steel. Maybe ten inches long, six wide. Tarnished brass latches clasped shut.

My hands, slick with a sudden nervous sweat, trembled as I reached into the cavity. My fingers closed around cool, solid metal. Surprisingly heavy.

Carefully, reverently, I lifted it out. A cloud of ancient dust puffed up, catching the thin light. Brushing away decades of accumulation from the lid revealed crude, almost desperate-looking initials etched into the tarnished surface: E.W.

Edward Wilson. The name slammed into my mind with the force of a physical blow.

Martha's late husband. The shelter's co-founder. The man who, Martha had said, died wanting to ensure its future, who'd hidden something somewhere only the 'right person' would find. My own breath caught again, this time with a sharp pang of dawning, staggering comprehension.

My breath caught. I surveyed the room. Still alone, just the background chorus of barks.

Max pressed against my side, a silent, furry witness. With uncertain hands, I worked the stiff latches. They released with a rusty snap. Heart hammering, I raised the lid.
Inside: a stack of papers, folded, yellowed, brittle. Official documents with First National Bank letterhead. I carefully unfolded the top sheets—"Maple Street Foundation Trust," a legal document, and correspondence to Edward Wilson about account parameters.

And then, tucked beneath, a single sheet drew my focus. A bank statement, ink faded to ghost grey. My pulse quickened as I read the bottom line: Ending Balance: $41,352.18.

Forty-one thousand dollars. From nearly twenty-five years ago. Untouched.

Accumulating interest. Hidden beneath the floor of Sam's old kennel.

"Air evaporated from my lungs. Adrenaline surged, hot and dizzying. Disbelief warred with dawning, earth-shattering understanding. This wasn't just paperwork. This *was* the answer. The shelter's desperate finances, the mountain of repairs that had seemed utterly beyond their reach, Martha's quiet struggle... and Sam. Sam guiding us here.

Max insisting, nudging, knowing. The shimmer of light, the double bark, the paw—it wasn't just about finding Max. It was about this. This time capsule. Holding the shelter's salvation. Hidden by the man who built it. Waiting.

My hands were definitely shaking now. Carefully, I refolded the documents, keeping the bank statement near the top. I closed the heavy lid, latches clicking shut with a sound that echoed in the sudden, ringing silence of my mind. This box held more than metal and paper. It held hope. Legacy. Sam's final, astonishing act of guidance.

Max nudged my hand gently, a near-silent whine escaping him, sensing the monumental weight of the moment. I looked down into his intelligent, knowing eyes—seeing not just a terrier mix, but a messenger, a partner, the living bridge Sam had sent.

"Okay, boy," I managed, my voice rough. "Okay. I understand."

With painstaking care, I lowered the heavy grate, wiggling it until it sat almost flush again, hiding its secret. Then, clutching the metal box tightly against my side under my sweatshirt, I stood on unsteady legs.

I had to tell Mom and Dad. Pastor John. But first... first, I needed the story behind this hidden legacy. And only one person held that key.

Martha.

"Come on, Max," I whispered, clipping the leash back on. He hesitated, looking back at kennel twenty one last time, then reluctantly followed me. His mission here was accomplished.

I walked back toward the reception area, the weight of the box both physical and profound—a tangible link to the past, a promise for the future, delivered through the enduring love of a dog I couldn't see, but whose presence I felt more strongly, more purposefully, than ever before. Max stayed close to my side, his role as messenger and guide more evident than ever.

CHAPTER 9:
HIDDEN TRUTHS

Martha Wilson's house occupied a corner of Cedar Lane, a tranquil street where ancient maples created a canopy overhead, their persistent roots forcing the sidewalk into undulating waves. The modest bungalow, wearing a coat of weathered cornflower blue, projected welcoming simplicity. Beside the entrance steps, a hand-carved wooden sign proclaimed "Wag More, Bark Less."

Max paced alongside me up the fractured concrete path, his customary exuberance replaced by attentive vigilance. Mom had insisted on bringing him—"He tends to create openings," she'd explained while helping me secure the heavy metal box in my backpack. We'd decided unanimously: consult Martha first, comprehend the complete history before expanding the circle beyond Pastor John.

Before my knuckles could meet the door, it opened inward. Martha appeared, arms dusted with flour, a kitchen towel draped across one shoulder. "Perfect timing," she welcomed us with genuine warmth. "And Max too! Marvelous." She motioned us inside. "Forgive the disarray—I bake when I'm anxious."

The house was gently perfumed with the comforting aroma of yeast and something sweet—baking, no doubt. Framed photos covered every surface—mostly animals, but some showed a younger Martha beside a tall, kind-eyed man with salt-and-pepper hair.

Edward. The living room beyond felt like her shelter office transposed: stacks of animal care books, handmade thank-you cards on the mantel.

"Sit anywhere the cat hasn't claimed," Martha gestured to a floral sofa where an orange tabby slept, bathed in afternoon sun. Max approached the cat cautiously, sniffed the air, then lay down respectfully nearby.

"That's Marmalade," Martha explained. "Fifteen, and firmly believes he's in charge." She returned from the kitchen with lemonade and cookies. "Thought you might enjoy something while we look through old albums." She settled into an armchair opposite me. "So," she began, "shelter history. Any particular aspect?"

Her directness cut through my prepared speeches. Straightforward felt best. "Actually," I began, heart starting to pound, "I'm curious how it was funded originally. If there were ever... special accounts? For its future?"

Something shifted behind Martha's eyes—not alarm, but recognition, settling into deep thought. She studied me over her glass. "An unusual question for someone your age."

"Dad's a contractor," I offered, the half-truth feeling thin. "Guess I picked up his interest in how things are built."

Martha set her glass down deliberately. "William," she said, her vision steady, "I sense something specific prompted this. Am I right?"

Taking a breath, I unzipped my backpack, withdrew the heavy, grimy box. "Yesterday," I started, voice steadier than I felt, "Max led me to kennel twenty."

"Sam's old kennel," Martha murmured..

"Yes. And to a loose drain grate." I placed the box on the coffee table between us. "I found this hidden underneath. Haven't shown anyone but my parents and Pastor John. Wanted to understand first."

Martha stared at the box, profound relief washing over her face. Her hands reached, hovered with a faint tremor, then pulled back. "I'd almost given up hope," she whispered.

"All these years... wondering."

"You knew about it?"

She nodded, gathering herself. "Of course. Edward—my husband—and I created the Maple Street Foundation. We hid these documents... when it became necessary."

"Necessary? To protect them from what?"

Martha rose, retrieved a framed photo from a bookshelf—a group standing proudly before a newer-looking shelter building, a "GRAND OPENING – 1983" banner strung across the front. "The original board," she explained, pointing. "Edward and me. Mayor Thompson—donated the land. The Chens—Molly's grandparents, our first vets. And this man—" her finger tapped a tall figure with a shrewd smile "—Victor Hargrove."

"Victor was a prominent businessman," she continued, her voice tightening slightly.

"Joined for prestige, made large donations. But his vision... clashed with ours. He wanted to operate like a business— sell purebreds, charge high fees, turn away 'unmarketable' animals."

"The opposite of what the shelter is," I said.

Precisely. When we resisted, Victor threatened a hostile takeover. His influence, his money... he might have succeeded." Martha's eyes, clouded with the old memory, drifted back to the metal box. "Edward, as financial director, created the foundation account as a safeguard. Transferred a significant portion of our reserves into a trust, accessible only under specific circumstances."

"And hid the proof," I finished.

"We had to. Victor was auditing, looking for leverage. Finding the foundation would have sealed his case." Martha sank back into her chair, the memory clearly painful. "Then Edward fell ill. Cancer, very fast. Before he died, he told me he'd secured the documents somewhere only the 'right person' would find them, when the time was right."

"He didn't say where?"

She shook her head. "Believed if I didn't know, I couldn't be forced to reveal it. He said, 'When the shelter faces its greatest need, the funds will surface.' I thought... I thought it was the illness talking. I searched everywhere afterwards. Never found it."

The story clicked into place. Not deception, but protection. Funds preserved for the shelter, not hidden from it. "So this account," I said, opening the box, carefully lifting the fragile bank statement, "it might still be active?"

"It should be. Edward set it up as a perpetual trust, accumulating interest. Principal accessible only by board supermajority, for capital improvements or emergencies."

Martha's eyes widened as she scanned the statement. "Over forty-one thousand... twenty-five years ago. Compound interest... it could be..."

"Enough," I breathed. "Enough to save the shelter."

"More than enough," she whispered back, hands trembling as she returned the statement to its sleeve. "All these years... fundraising, budget cuts, worrying... and the answer was waiting."

"Waiting for the right guide," I corrected.

Wonder dawned on Martha's face. "But how did you know? That specific drain? That kennel?"

The question hung there. I owed her the full truth. "I think Sam guided us," I said simply. "Max, really. But led by Sam."

Martha acknowledged, no trace of disbelief. "Sam," she repeated. "Of course. It would be Sam."

Her immediate acceptance startled me. "You believe that?"

"William, work with animals long enough, you learn some transcend the ordinary. Sam was special from day one—a stray found near the highway, no ID, yet preternaturally calm, unnervingly intelligent." She reached for a worn photo album. "Meant to show you these."

She opened it near the beginning. There he was. Sam as a puppy—white fur smudged, one ear flopped, those intelligent eyes meeting the camera directly.

"Standard arrival photos," Martha explained. "But Sam's were... different. Look." She turned the page. A series of shots. In each, Sam seemed to be looking past the camera, attention fixed on empty air with that same focused intensity Max sometimes showed. In the final photo, a strange blur of light partly obscured the frame.

"The volunteer swore she saw something misty, white, moving around him that day. Whatever it was, it didn't show up with any real definition on film. We dismissed it."

Martha studied the image. "But Sam always seemed... aware. Barking at empty corners. Sitting attentively beside elderly visitors, listening to unheard conversations."

"You think he could see... spirits?" The word felt clumsy, inadequate.

Martha considered it seriously. "Wouldn't have used that word then. Now? Perhaps. Or 'energy,' maybe. The essence of those passed but not entirely gone." Her thoughtful eyes found Max, now positioned near the window, bathed in afternoon light. "Some animals are more attuned. Max, I believe, shares that sensitivity."

As if on cue, Max sat taller, attention locking onto a point near the ceiling where dust motes danced in a sunbeam. Ears pricked, head tilted.

"This wasn't your first experience with this kind of dog, was it?" I asked, suddenly certain.

Martha smiled softly, rising to retrieve another album from a higher shelf. "No," she admitted, settling back with the weathered book. "My first was Archie. Had him as a girl in the '60s." She opened to a yellowed photo of a teenage Martha with a border collie. "Archie would bark at empty corners, lead me to people who needed help before they knew they needed it."

She turned a page. "Then came Benson, when Edward and I first married." A German shepherd mix with intelligent eyes. "He's actually why we started the shelter. One winter morning, he dragged us three miles through snow to an abandoned barn. Found six puppies, nearly frozen. Wouldn't leave until we took them all."

Martha traced the image with a weathered finger. "Edward began noticing patterns.

Certain animals—not many, maybe one in hundreds— seemed connected to something beyond ordinary perception. They'd find the exact people who needed them, know things they couldn't possibly know."

"Like Sam finding us," I murmured.

"Precisely. Edward called them 'threshold beings'—creatures who could perceive beyond the veil between worlds." Her eyes met mine directly. "He believed they came with purpose. Not just as companions, but as guides."

Max turned his head sharply toward the window, alert, tracking something invisible across the yard.

"Don't you find it strange?" I asked. "That Sam was placed in that specific kennel? That Max led us right to the box?"

Martha's expression grew distant. "Edward spent his final night at the shelter sitting beside kennel twenty, talking to empty air. When I asked him what he was doing, he said, 'Making arrangements.' I thought it was the medication." She shook her head slowly. "Now I wonder if he knew. If that space has always been special. A threshold."

"He does that at home," I told her. "Near Sam's grave. His old bed."

"Looking across the veil," Martha stated, as if it were simple fact. Seeing my confusion, she added, "My grandmother's term. The membrane between worlds. Thin in places. Some can peer across."

The conversation had veered far from finances, yet felt essential.

"The day after Sam died," I began, "I saw a cloud like his face. Smiling. Then the flower grew on his grave—instantly, stays dry in rain, doesn't wilt."

Martha listened, expression open, accepting.

"At first, I thought grief was making me see things. But then others saw them too. Mom, Lyn, even Dad. Pastor John thinks Sam might be communicating." I gestured to the box.

"Finding this... feels like the point."

"A final act of service," Martha murmured. "Saving the place that once saved him."

The phrase resonated. Sam, the *protector.* From aggressive dogs, from that time Mom left the oven on before our weekend trip and Sam wouldn't stop barking until Dad checked it, from countless unnoticed dangers. Even now, protecting not just us, but all the animals needing this place.

A disturbance passed through the sunbeam near Max. For an instant—so brief I almost doubted it—a familiar silhouette formed against the wall. White, ephemeral, undeniably Sam. Max's tail thumped once, deliberately, against the floor. Acknowledgment.
Martha followed my eyes, her breath catching. "Did you see—"

"Yes," I whispered. "He's here."

We sat in reverent silence, acknowledging the unseen guidance that had brought us to this moment, to this shared understanding. Then, gradually, the silhouette faded, leaving only afternoon stillness and dancing dust motes.

"Well," Martha said finally, practicality returning, though her voice held emotion. "Next steps. This money needs proper reintegration."

"Mom suggested Pastor John," I offered. "He knows people at the bank."

Wise. We'll need to convene the board too—all five of us." Seeing my surprise, a wry smile touched her lips. "Yes, small these days. Myself, Dr. Chen—Molly's father—Pastor John, Mrs. Jenkins from the auxiliary, and the Mayor, ex officio.

"Three out of five already agree," I observed, doing the quick math. "That should be enough."

"Especially since three are already involved in fundraising. This will feel like..." she hesitated.

"Providence," I supplied.

"Exactly." Martha rose, gathering the documents carefully. "I should secure these. Make copies this time. Mind waiting?"

While she worked in her office, I examined the living room photos again. Decades of dedication. One photo drew me— Martha kneeling beside a white dog, not Sam, but similar. The frame back was loose; a note had slipped partway out. Compelled, I slid it free enough to read: *Archie – 1975-1989.* The first who showed me they could see across. Archie. Special too. A lineage of sentinels?

Martha returned with a manila envelope. I replaced the photo, the note unseen. "Been thinking," she said, handing me the box. "Why kennel twenty?"

"Sam stayed there," I reminded her.

"Yes, but more. That kennel... always felt different." She settled beside me on the sofa; Marmalade instantly reclaimed her lap. "Over the years, animals housed there often found exactly the right homes—families facing challenges those specific animals seemed uniquely suited for."

"Like Sam finding us," I murmured.

"Precisely. A matchmaking spirit, we joked." Martha stroked the cat. "Edward spent his final days at the shelter, his choice. Wanted to die surrounded by the animals. The night before he passed, the volunteer saw him sitting beside kennel twenty for hours... talking to empty air." The implication hung there—Edward entrusting the shelter's future to whatever presence resided in that specific space.

"And now Sam led us back," I said. "Right when the shelter needed saving."

"Full circle," Martha mused. "Edward believed there were no accidents, only patterns we hadn't yet recognized."

Max left the window, pressing gently against my leg. Outside, clouds gathered, dappening the light. Through the window, they formed an unusual pattern—not Sam, but an open book, pages turning in unseen wind, before slowly dispersing.

"Should get home," I said, zipping the box safely into my backpack. "Mom will want to know. We should meet with Pastor John tomorrow."

CHAPTER 10:

WHISPERS OF DOUBT

Night had fallen by the time I returned home, the metal box a significant weight against my back. The journey from Martha's house had seemed longer, each pedal stroke deliberate as my mind processed everything she'd shared about Edward Wilson, Victor Hargrove, and the shelter's hidden history. Streetlights cast long shadows as I navigated familiar roads made somehow different by the treasure I carried.

Mom waited at the kitchen table, a mug of cooling tea before her. Her expression brightened as I entered, eyes fixed on my backpack.

"You found something," she said, her voice barely above a whisper, her eyes already fixed on the grimy outline of the box through the opening of my backpack.

"More than something," I replied, carefully extracting the heavy metal box and placing it on the table between us with a soft thud. "Everything."

Mom leaned forward, her breath catching. Her hand, when she reached out, trembled slightly before her fingers traced the crude E.W. initials etched into the tarnished lid. A look of profound, almost disbelieving awe settled on her face, as if she were beholding a long-lost sacred relic.

"Edward Wilson," she breathed, rather than spoke. "Martha confirmed it?"

As I spoke, Mom carefully opened the box. Her hands, usually so quick and efficient, moved with an uncharacteristic slowness as she spread the brittle documents across the wooden surface, treating each yellowed page with the delicacy of ancient scripture.

Her eyes scanned the faded bank statement, widening almost imperceptibly. She traced the bottom line with a fingertip, her lips parting slightly.

"Over forty thousand," she breathed, her voice a mixture of disbelief and dawning wonder. "And that was decades ago."

"Compound interest," I agreed, the mathematical concept suddenly profound in its implications. "Martha thinks it could be enough to save the shelter completely. All those renovations Dad calculated—the kennel floors, drainage system, ventilation—it would cover everything."

"And Martha had no idea where these documents were?" Mom asked, her expression caught between wonder and caution.

"Edward never told her exactly. Just said they were hidden somewhere only the 'right person' would find when the shelter needed them most." The implication hung between us—I had been that right person, or rather, Sam through Max had guided me to become that person.

Mom gathered the documents carefully, returning them to the box. "We should call Pastor John first thing tomorrow.

He'll know how to approach the bank correctly."

"That's what Martha suggested too."

Mom's hands lingered on the closed box. "This is extraordinary, Will. Beyond coincidence. Sam led you directly to this, through Max."

The mention of Sam sent a flicker of something unexpected through me—not comfort or confirmation, but a whisper of doubt. The evening's shadows suddenly seemed deeper, the kitchen less certain. Standing abruptly, I mumbled about needing sleep and retreated upstairs, leaving Mom's concerned gaze behind.

In my bedroom, reality felt suddenly fragile. I sat at my desk, journal open before me, staring at weeks of careful observations—cloud patterns, weather conditions, timestamps of each sighting and manifestation. The box discovery fit perfectly into our developing narrative—Sam guiding us to save the place that once saved him. A beautiful, meaningful story.

But was it true? Or were we simply connecting random dots, imposing meaning onto coincidence with the desperate energy of grief?

My pencil hovered over the blank journal page. What would I write? That we'd discovered financial salvation hidden in a rusty box beneath a drain grate, guided by a dead dog communicating through clouds and flowers? The rational part of my brain—the part Ms. Winters encouraged in math class, the part that understood statistical probability and confirmation bias—recoiled at the thought.

The white flower. The cloud formations. Max's behaviors. The box hidden precisely where Sam had once lived. Each individually could be explained away. A rare botanical anomaly. Pareidolia seeing faces in random patterns. Animal behavior mimicking previous training. A logical hiding place for important documents.

Together, though? All converging into this coherent narrative? What were the odds?

I crossed to the window, watching clouds obscure the quarter moon. No shapes tonight. No messages. Just atmospheric water vapor drifting on air currents.

Sleep proved elusive. I lay atop my covers, mind spinning through explanations, rationalizations, doubts. What if tomorrow the bank representative laughed at these ancient documents? What if the account had been closed decades ago? What if we were building hope on vapor as insubstantial as those clouds?

Around midnight, restlessness drove me outside. The grass felt cool beneath my bare feet as I crossed to the oak tree. Against the deep velvet of the night, the white flower pulsed with a gentle, internal light, its petals perfect as ever. I knelt beside it, fingers hovering just above its surface, remembering how it had responded to Lyn's touch, to Pastor John's.

"Am I imagining all this?" I whispered. "Are you really here, or am I just... desperate to believe you are?"

No answer came. Just night sounds—distant traffic, rustling leaves, a neighbor's wind chime. For weeks I'd interpreted such ordinary moments as meaningful, but what if they were just... ordinary?

A twig snapped behind me. Max stood there, his approach otherwise silent on the dewy grass. His eyes caught the moonlight, reflecting it back with unnerving intelligence. He padded forward, settling beside me, pressing warmly against my side.

"What if we're wrong, Max?" I murmured, finding strange comfort in confessing my doubts to him. "What if the box is just an old box that happened to be hidden where you led me? What if Pastor John and the banker tell us tomorrow that the account doesn't exist anymore, or the money's gone?"

Max tilted his head, regarding me steadily in the moonlight. Then, with deliberate movement, he placed his paw on my knee—that familiar gesture of comfort Sam had perfected years ago.

"That's just training," I told him, though my throat tightened. "Lots of dogs do that. Doesn't prove anything."

Max met my look with a steady, unwavering intensity for a moment longer before slowly turning toward the flower. He approached it, sniffing carefully before looking back at me. As I watched, a single dewdrop slid from a petal, catching the moonlight as it fell to the earth. Not withering, not dying—simply releasing something no longer needed.

The night air shifted, and for a fleeting instant, an almost imperceptible whisper of Sam's scent brushed past—clean fur, that unmistakably Sam-like gentle presence. Then it was gone. Was it memory? Imagination? Or had he truly been there?

I remained beneath the oak for nearly an hour, Max silently beside me. The doubt didn't disappear—if anything, it crystallized into more precise questions. What did it mean if Sam was guiding us? What did it mean if he wasn't? Did the difference actually matter if the outcome—helping the shelter, bringing our family closer, giving purpose to our grief—remained the same?

Perhaps this was the real test of faith—not blindly believing without question, but choosing to move forward despite questions. Seeing meaning even while acknowledging uncertainty.

Upstairs again, I found my cloud journal where I'd left it. Turning to a fresh page, I wrote simply:

Is doubt the opposite of faith, or part of it? Tomorrow we'll meet with Pastor John and the banker. Either the funds exist or they don't. Either Sam is guiding us or we're finding our own way through grief. Either way, we're changing. We're healing. We're rediscovering purpose. *Maybe* that's the miracle that matters most.

I slept then, a deeper rest than I'd known in days. No dreams of Sam, no visions, just quiet darkness and renewal.

Dawn arrived with gentle insistence, sunlight streaming through my window. Mom's voice called me to breakfast, where Dad had already spread the documents across the kitchen table like ancient maps to a lost world. Property deeds, trust agreements, the fragile bank statement—Edward Wilson's hidden legacy, unearthed.

Max patrolled beneath our chairs, a furry, four-legged reminder of the guidance that led us here, occasionally pressing his nose against my leg. Whatever today brought—confirmation or disappointment—I realized we had already found something precious. Connection. Purpose. The belief that love, once given, continued in ways we might never fully understand.

Facts would soon replace faith—for better or worse. And somehow, I felt ready for either outcome.

CHAPTER 11:

THE UNVEILING

Morning sunlight streamed into the kitchen, illuminating the documents spread across the table like ancient maps to a lost world. Property deeds, trust agreements, the fragile bank statement— Edward Wilson's hidden legacy, unearthed. Max patrolled beneath our chairs, a furry, four-legged reminder of the guidance that led us here, occasionally pressing his nose against my leg.

"Still can't wrap my head around this," Dad said, examining a faded paper, his contractor's eye noting details beyond the text. "Hidden for over twenty years. Under a drain grate."

"Hiding in plain sight," Mom observed, pouring coffee. "Smart, really. Who'd look there?"

Lyn, still in pajamas, leaned closer to the bank statement. "So this money... it just grew? All by itself?"

"If the account's still active," Dad cautioned, though his voice lacked its usual skeptical edge. "Need to verify before getting hopes up."

I traced the faded account number. "Martha thinks it should be. A perpetual trust."

"Smart man, Edward Wilson," Dad murmured, admiration

clear in his tone.

"The question is how to proceed," Mom said, setting down her teapot. "Martha suggested meeting with Pastor John first?"

"She was calling him yesterday. Probably this afternoon," I said.

Dad checked his watch. "Should be able to make it after three. Got that lumber supplier meeting this morning." The shelter renovations—still proceeding as if fundraising was the only path. The irony was thick.

"Should we tell people?" Lyn asked abruptly. "About the money? Everyone's working so hard."

It was the question that had kept me up half the night. Car washes, bake sales, pledge drives—the whole town rallying. Would this discovery deflate them?

"Transparency is important," Mom mused, "but timing matters. We need confirmation first."

"And frame it right," Dad added, surprising me with his grasp of the emotional dynamics. "Make sure everyone knows their efforts still count. Still help the shelter operate better."

"Like the Max Fund!" Lyn suggested, brightening.

"The what?" I asked.

"The Max Fund!" she repeated, enthusiasm bubbling. "If the foundation covers repairs, the fundraising money could go into a special account! Help families adopt who can't afford it, or pay for special vet treatments! Named after Max, 'cause he found it!"

The idea landed perfectly—practical, compassionate, honoring past and present. Even Max seemed to perk up at his name.

"That's... actually brilliant, Lyn," Dad admitted, bringing a rare flush of pleasure to her cheeks. "A sustainable way to extend the mission."

"Gives purpose to community efforts," Mom agreed. "Doesn't make them seem pointless."

As they discussed logistics, my gaze drifted outside. The oak stood sentinel, the white flower glowing softly beneath it. Beyond, high, wispy clouds caught the sunlight like spun gold. For a heartbeat, they seemed to align—was that a fleeting image of a dog running joyfully?—before dissolving back into randomness. Or perhaps not randomness. A sense of approval, of rightness, settled over me.

The phone rang, startling us. Mom answered, listened intently, expression shifting. "That was Martha," she reported after hanging up. "Pastor John can meet at the church office.
Three-thirty. He's bringing someone from First National. Confidentially."

"Moving fast," Dad observed, rising. "Good. I'll be there." He paused, resting a hand briefly on my shoulder, a gesture no longer awkward but natural. "Good work, Will.

Finding this... it's going to make a real difference."

The hours until the meeting crawled with excruciating slowness. I attempted to distract myself with my cloud journal, methodically cataloging formations, weather conditions, and corresponding events. My hand traced the most recent entry—the book-shaped clouds that had appeared yesterday. Flipping back through pages, the progression became striking: random shapes giving way to increasingly specific formations, each coinciding with critical discoveries or decisions. The patterns felt undeniable now—these weren't random meteorological phenomena but deliberate messages appearing at pivotal moments. Guidance from beyond ordinary perception.

"Making progress?" Mom appeared in the doorway, two mugs of tea in hand. A welcome interruption.

"Just reviewing the timeline," I explained, accepting the steaming mug. "It's pretty remarkable when you see it all documented."

She settled on the edge of my bed, peering at the open journal. "It really is," she agreed, finger tracing the careful chronology. "From that first smile in the clouds to..." she paused, shaking her head with a mixture of wonder and acceptance, "...to finding a forty-year-old trust that could save an entire shelter. Not exactly subtle guidance, is it?"

That pulled a genuine laugh from me—the first in days. "Sam never was big on subtlety. Remember when he'd bring his leash and drop it directly on anyone's foot when he wanted a walk?"

"Or how he'd sit beside the refrigerator staring at us until someone remembered his dinner time," Mom added, her smile tinged with both sadness and affection. "Always made his intentions perfectly clear."

We shared a comfortable silence, sipping tea and remembering. The small moment of normalcy amid the extraordinary events felt like another gift.

Eventually, Mom checked her watch. "Better start getting ready. Pastor John appreciates punctuality."

With a quiet sigh, I closed the journal, the weight of all we'd experienced pressing in on me.. "Do you think the bank guy—Francis?—will believe any of this?"

Mom considered this. "He doesn't need to understand the full story. Just the documents and the legal aspects." She paused at the door. "Though I've found that people often surprise you with what they're willing to believe when faced with enough evidence."

By three o'clock, our family—plus Max, whose presence felt absolutely non-negotiable—gathered with Mom outside the church. Dad arrived last, direct from a job site, but had taken time to change into a clean shirt. Even his skepticism had evolved into something closer to cautious acceptance.

Pastor John greeted us in the church conference room. Martha sat at one end of the long table, looking composed but expectant. Max made a deliberate circuit of the room before settling near the window, watchful.

"Thank you all for coming," Pastor John began. "Francis

should be here momentarily."

Martha caught my eye, looking toward Max. "I've been thinking about our conversation, William. About certain animals being... attuned."

"Remembering something else?"

"Realizing something," she corrected gently. "Over the years, kennel twenty residents often found homes with families needing specific support. We joked it had a matchmaking spirit." Her view grew distant. "Edward spent his final days at the shelter. The night before he passed, a volunteer saw him sitting beside kennel twenty for hours... talking to empty air." She looked back at me. "Perhaps entrusting its energy?"

Before I could respond, the door opened. Francis Chen entered—slim, sharp suit, wire-rimmed glasses, carrying a leather portfolio. He bore a resemblance to Molly's father but radiated banker's efficiency.

"Apologies," he said, setting the portfolio down. "Some records required special access."

Introductions were made, though most knew each other. Francis greeted Molly, who had joined us at Pastor John's invitation, with familial warmth before turning to business.

"The Edward Wilson Shelter Trust," he began, removing documents. "Remarkable. When Pastor John called, I assumed an error—the trust has been dormant for decades."

"But it exists?" Dad asked, voicing the core question.

Francis allowed a brief, meticulously controlled smile to touch his lips. "Oh yes, Mr. Thomas. It very much exists." He turned his laptop, displaying a balance sheet. The final number silenced the room.

$127,846.59

"Original deposit plus accumulated interest," Francis explained coolly. "Edward Wilson's investment instructions were unusually prescient."

Martha pressed a hand to her heart, tears glistening. "Edward always did think long-term," she whispered.

Across the table, Mom's hand flew to her mouth, not unlike Martha's, but her eyes—wide and shining—immediately sought mine, a look of such profound, joyous disbelief and gratitude passing between us that it warmed me to my core. She then reached for Dad's hand, her fingers interlacing tightly with his, a silent testament to the answered prayers and the incredible journey that had brought them to this moment.

"Access requires board supermajority approval," Francis continued, "for capital improvements or emergencies. This situation unquestionably qualifies."

"What's the process?" Dad inquired, his mind already shifting toward implementation.

"Formal board vote, notarized documentation, submission to the trust department. I recommend including an explanatory statement regarding the rediscovery circumstances." Francis adjusted his glasses with practiced precision. "I've prepared all necessary paperwork."

"Three board members are present," Martha noted—herself, Pastor John, Francis (apparently serving in some official capacity). "Dr. Chen has approved by phone. That constitutes our required supermajority." Events had clearly advanced rapidly behind the scenes.

"Then let's proceed," Pastor John concluded.

What followed was a brief, formal board meeting layered over years of community history and unseen guidance. Martha moved to access the funds, Pastor John seconded, approval was unanimous. As Francis guided Martha through signing, my attention snagged on Max. He'd moved from the window to stand near an empty corner, posture alert, eyes fixed on something unseen.

Just then, I felt it—a palpable shift in the room's atmosphere. The low hum of the building's HVAC system seemed to abruptly cease, plunging the conference room into a profound, expectant silence. A pressure against my ears made them pop gently, like descending in an airplane. Across the table, Mom pressed her fingers to her temples, while Pastor John sat straighter in his chair. Dad shifted uncomfortably, casting a puzzled glance at the windows.

"Did the barometric pressure just change?" Francis Chen asked, adjusting his collar, his professional composure momentarily slipping.

"Something's different," Dad agreed, rubbing the back of his neck.

Martha's attention, however, was fixed on the documents. "Do you smell that?" she asked.

I inhaled deeply. A familiar scent washed over me—clean dog, fresh earth, and something indefinably Sam. I looked towards Mom, and her eyes met mine instantly, a tiny, almost imperceptible smile playing on her lips as she gave a slow, deliberate nod. It wasn't just confirmation; it was a shared acknowledgment of his presence, a silent *"he's here with us"* passing between us. Pastor John closed his eyes briefly, his expression serene.

"Smells like..." Dad hesitated, frowning slightly. "Like outside after rain."

Francis seemed not to notice, already reviewing the clauses. But as his fingers traced the documents, something remarkable happened. The faded ink on the pages appeared to darken before my eyes, becoming more legible, as if the decades-old writing was somehow refreshing itself beneath his touch.

"These documents are remarkably well-preserved," Francis commented, unaware of the subtle transformation I was witnessing.

A strange sensation traveled up my arm as I touched the corner of a page—a delicate tingle, like a gentle static charge, coupled with the barely perceptible thrum of a purring cat. Mom, who had also reached out to steady a different document, drew in a quick, sharp breath, her eyes widening slightly before flicking to meet mine again. This time, her look was less about shared knowledge and more about a shared, startled wonder, a silent question of *"You too?*" But Dad and Francis continued their discussion about account access procedures, apparently unaffected.

Pastor John caught my eye, a knowing look passing between us. He sensed it too—Sam's spirit at work, manifesting in ways only some of us could perceive. Not everyone was attuned to it.

Under the table, I felt Max press against my leg, his body trembling slightly, alert and aware. A silent confirmation that something extraordinary was happening, invisible to some but undeniably real.

When Francis eventually picked up the pen to sign the final authorization, his hand, which had trembled slightly when touching the papers, moved with remarkable steadiness, the pen flowing across the page as if guided.

"Funds available immediately," he announced, professional tone restored, though his eyes held a new awareness. "No waiting period."

As the meeting concluded, the unusual phenomena gradually subsided, leaving behind transformed understanding—at least for those who had noticed them. As we stepped outside the bank, a sudden breeze encircled us, carrying a distinct jingling sound, like metal tags against a collar. Dad halted mid-sentence, scanning the area.

"Did you hear that?" he asked, genuine puzzlement in his voice.

Before anyone could answer, a white feather descended from the clear blue sky, twisting in that inexplicable breeze, settling directly at my feet. I bent, retrieving it—soft, intact, and carrying that same familiar scent. No birds overhead. No rational explanation.

"Thank you," I whispered, tucking it carefully into my pocket. Another sign. Confirmation.

Max, waiting patiently by the car, barked twice—that distinct, affirmative rhythm—before hopping inside. Messenger and receiver, mission advanced, guided by a love stronger than death.

In the days that followed, Dad began sketching preliminary renovation plans while Martha started the paperwork process to access the funds. "Realistically," Dad explained over dinner that night, "we're looking at a three to four month timeline—permits, approvals, actual construction."A thin, knowing smile touched his lips. 'Even with all the willing hands offering to help, some things just take time."

I nodded, thinking about how Sam's guidance had felt so immediate, so urgent. But now I understood—he'd set things in motion exactly when they needed to start, allowing enough time for the shelter's license renewal deadline. Not rushed, but perfectly timed.

Just like Sam had always seemed to know precisely when we needed him most.

CHAPTER 12:

TRANSFORMATION

The crack of a hammer shattering old concrete echoed through the bright May morning—a definitive sound of beginning. Dad stood amidst a crew of volunteer contractors—friends he'd rallied—directing the first phase of renovation, pride radiating from his stance. Near the temporary fence separating onlookers from the worksite, I watched years of weariness start to fall away under purposeful hands.

"It's really happening," Lyn breathed beside me, fingers laced through the wire mesh.

"Weeks ago, we didn't even know..."

"Sam knew," I murmured, the conviction solid now. "He planned this."

Warm sunshine bathed the scene, glinting off tools. A surprising crowd had gathered—not just volunteers, but townspeople drawn by the story of the shelter's miraculous turnaround, transforming a construction kickoff into a community event.

Martha moved through the clusters, accepting congratulations but deftly redirecting praise toward "the remarkable Thomas family" and "Edward's foresight." Only the inner circle knew the full truth: a white dog's enduring love had guided us here.

Max maintained vigilant attention at my feet, observing with analytical focus. Since uncovering the documents, his demeanor had evolved beyond typical pet behavior into something resembling conscious participation. When demolition equipment brought down a substantial section of concrete flooring, his ears stiffened to attention, head pivoting deliberately toward the seemingly unoccupied space beside us.

"You perceive him too?" I murmured, lowering myself beside Max. "Is he monitoring our progress?"

Max's tail traced a single arc across the construction dust—a deliberate, unhurried gesture, almost ritual in nature. From my crouched perspective, the chain-link fence created interwoven shadow patterns across the ground. One particular shadow appeared momentarily more defined, more dimensional—distinctly canine in form, though cast by no visible entity. An unexpected coolness, reminiscent of a moist canine nose, made contact with my cheek, immediately followed by warmth comparable to Sam's breath when rousing me from sleep.

Tangible. Unmistakably Sam. My breath caught sharply.

"Will?" Mom appeared beside me, concern in her eyes. "Okay?"

I straightened, finding words difficult. "Just... felt him. Right here."

A look of knowing empathy smoothed the concern from her

features, immediate understanding dawning in her eyes. "Felt it too," she admitted, her voice a low murmur meant only for me. "Near the big oak they're saving. That familiar warmth." Her shared perception sent a shiver of confirmation through me. He was here. Moving among us.

"Mrs. Thomas?" Martha approached, clipboard ready. "Albert needs you on the cat room plans. Light fixtures."

As Mom left with Martha, I saw Molly Chen crossing the parking lot, camera bag slung over one shoulder, large display board tucked under the other. The science fair. I'd almost forgotten.

"Preliminary judging at noon," she reminded me, slightly breathless. "Thought we should set up early."

Our display represented weeks of work—cloud photos, weather data, pattern analysis, and carefully termed "synchronistic phenomena." Tomorrow, the district fair. Today, the school gym showcase.

"Backpack's in the car," I told her. "Observation journals."

Crossing toward our sedan, a flash of white near the property edge caught my eye. There, sprouting beside the shelter's main sign, bloomed a single white flower— identical to the one on *Sam's grave*. Its petals gleamed, impossibly pristine despite the swirling construction dust. It hadn't been there yesterday. I was certain.

"Molly," I called, gesturing her over. "Look."

She joined me, scientific curiosity overriding surprise.

Camera out, she photographed it methodically, multiple angles, while wonder widened her eyes. "Physically identical to the grave specimen," she noted, kneeling. "Same petal configuration, golden center.

Appearing without normal growth, in undisturbed soil."

"He's marking territory," I suggested, the thought clicking into place with startling clarity.

"Establishing a boundary."

Molly glanced up sharply. "Interesting analogy. Territorial marking..."

"But if the flowers are just a form his influence takes," I reasoned, "then maybe animal behavior applies. Creating a protected space around the shelter." It felt right. Like Sam extending his guardianship.

"Documenting this," Molly decided, rising. "Consistent with the pattern."

Retrieving my backpack, I felt torn—eager for the fair, reluctant to leave the tangible transformation here. Dad noticed us preparing to leave, crossing over, work gloves in his back pocket.

"Heading to school?" he asked, wiping sweat from his brow.

"Science fair setup," I explained.

A thoughtful look crossed Dad's face, and he inclined his head, his expression holding a sincere interest that was indeed a rarity regarding my schoolwork. "Your cloud project?

The one... involving Sam?" His directness still felt new.

"We're calling it 'Pattern Recognition in Atmospheric Phenomena and Synchronistic Events'," Molly supplied smoothly.

"Smart," Dad approved. "Scientific, but leaves room for the... inexplicable." He glanced toward the ongoing demolition. "Like this. On paper, just a renovation. The reality..." He trailed off. We understood.

"Back this afternoon," I promised.

Dad laughed, genuine warmth in the sound. "Plenty to do. Just beginning." He hesitated, voice lowering slightly. "You know, Will, proud of how you've handled all this.

Navigating the practical and the... other stuff... with clear eyes."

His rare praise landed with unexpected weight. Before I could respond, he squeezed my shoulder and returned to his crew, shouting instructions about salvaging oak trim.

"Your father's perspective has shifted," Molly observed as we walked to her mom's car.

"Sam made it pretty hard to ignore," I replied with a faint smile.

"Like someone else I know," Molly returned, glancing

playfully at Max, who had appeared silently beside us.

"He's coming too?"

"Cleared with Principal Winters," Molly confirmed with satisfaction. "Relevant to methodology."

Mrs. Chen greeted us warmly, securing Max in the back without question. As we drove away, I looked back—the busy site, the gathering supporters, that single white flower standing sentinel.

The gymnasium hummed with activity, transformed from athletic arena to scientific showcase. Student projects lined the perimeter in neat rows—the standard volcanoes and battery-powered motors mingling with more sophisticated experiments on water purification and solar efficiency.

Our three-panel display commanded attention in the center section: the left panel featuring meticulous cloud photography and statistical analysis; the center outlining our unique methodology and preliminary findings; the right dedicated to "environmental anomalies"—carefully worded documentation of the flower's extraordinary resilience and characteristics that defied typical biology, complete with microscope slides of its cellular structure.

As we made final adjustments, I caught snippets of conversation from passing students:

"Thomas and Chen went full X-Files..."
"...heard they're claiming to communicate with ghosts or something..."
"...Ms. Winters actually sponsored this?"

Molly remained unfazed by the murmurs, methodically arranging our documentation binders with scientific precision. "Expected skepticism," she whispered, not looking up.

"Actually validates our methodological controls."

Max sat beside our display with remarkable composure, occasionally tracking movement but mostly maintaining a dignified stillness that seemed intentional—as if he understood his role in this academic presentation. Several teachers glanced his way with raised eyebrows, though no one challenged his presence.

"Impressive scope," Ms. Winters commented, materializing beside us after completing her initial circuit of the exhibits. Her eyes paused, lingering with a thoughtful intensity on the cloud photographs displaying Sam's silhouette, her expression revealing neither dismissal nor immediate acceptance. "Significant research investment evident."

"Thank you," Molly responded with professional composure. "We've attempted rigorous documentation protocols while maintaining intellectual openness toward phenomena currently beyond established scientific explanation frameworks."

Ms. Winters' lips quirked slightly—not quite a smile, but a gesture suggesting intellectual respect. "Studying things science hasn't yet explained, using scientific methodology to approach the unexplained. Paradoxically sound approach." Her attention shifted to Max, who sat with almost unnatural stillness. "And this gentleman's official research capacity?"

"Key variable," I confirmed, finding unexpected confidence in her receptiveness. "He consistently demonstrates awareness of anomalous phenomena, often detecting manifestations before human observation registers them."

"Utilizing cross-species perception," she nodded thoughtfully. "Canids possess sensory capabilities beyond human parameters—particularly auditory and olfactory."

"And possibly perceptual frameworks less constrained by existing belief systems," Molly added carefully.

Understanding flickered in Ms. Winters' expression—something deeper than mere academic interest. "Good science begins precisely where certainty ends," she stated, her tone suggesting personal conviction beneath professional assessment. "History demonstrates repeatedly that investigating phenomena others dismiss often precedes significant discovery." She adjusted her glasses. "I'll be interested in the judges' response."

As she moved to the next display, I exchanged a look with Molly. "Did she just basically validate our whole approach?"

"More precisely, she acknowledged its methodological legitimacy," Molly replied, though her eyes shone with barely contained excitement. "Coming from Winters, that's practically a standing ovation."

The unexpected support bolstered my confidence as the first round of judges approached, clipboards in hand. Whatever happened next, we'd already achieved something significant—bringing the inexplicable into the realm of serious inquiry, creating a framework where Sam's continuing influence could be acknowledged within academic parameters.

Other students cast curious glances. Josh Miller paused, condescension warring with intrigue. "Magical dog clouds," he observed, scanning the photos. "Bold."

"Pattern recognition," Molly corrected coolly. "Correlational analysis."

Witnessed phenomena?" Josh pressed, pointing. I gestured to the panel detailing the flower's unchanging state and its unusual defiance of normal botanical cycles.

"Huh," Josh sounded genuinely puzzled. "Actually... weirdly interesting." He glanced at Max. "He's part of it?"

"Demonstrates statistically significant predictive response," Molly stated flatly. Josh retreated, looking back, confused.

Judges began circulating. Dad arrived, flushed from work; Mom slipped in after coordinating with Martha. Their being there anchored me.

Our turn. Three judges: Mr. Peterson (physics), Dr. Chen (Molly's dad, chemistry), and Martha Wilson (community).

"Pattern Recognition... Synchronistic Events," Mr. Peterson read, skepticism clear.

"We began with a focused question," Molly launched into our presentation. We guided them through—Molly on data, me on observed patterns and correlations. Max sat inquisitively, ears occasionally twitching.

Dr. Chen studied the flower slides. "Unusual cellular structures," he murmured. "No match in standard references."

Martha focused on implications. "Cloud formations preceding discoveries," she observed. "Conclusions?"

Molly and I exchanged a look. How far? "Data suggests a non-random relationship," I began carefully. "Statistical improbability indicates an organizing influence beyond standard meteorology."

"In simpler terms," Molly added, "something—or someone—appears to be communicating."

Mr. Peterson opened his mouth to challenge, but froze as Max abruptly sat at full attention, ears pricked, gaze locked on the gym entrance.

The main doors swung open. Mom and Dad stood framed there, but behind them, something extraordinary happened. The gymnasium air suddenly became charged, like before a thunderstorm. A distinct electric sensation swept across the room, causing the hairs on everyone's arms to stand up. It moved with palpable purpose across the polished floor, directly toward our display. The phenomenon expanded, creating a perfect circle that encompassed our project, the judges, Molly, Max, and me.

Within this space, the air grew noticeably warmer, comforting, familiar. Sound seemed to bend around us, creating a pocket of sacred quiet amid the gymnasium's usual echoes. More than just warmth—an almost physical wave of profound peace washed over me, silencing the frantic beat of my own heart, a feeling so pure and buoyant it felt like Sam himself was right there, enveloping us in his essence.

I risked a glance at Molly; her face, usually so composed during presentations, was pale, her eyes wide and fixed on the swirling shadows around us, her scientific notebook forgotten in her lap.

Around our table, wispy shadows shifted without source, flowing momentarily into shapes suggesting a joyful canine form weaving between us. The shadows deepened briefly, gaining substance, though remaining transparent. The rest of the gymnasium fell utterly silent, a held breath in the face of the inexplicable. Everyone stared. For twenty seconds, this shared vision, so contrary to every known physical law, and the feeling of serene presence held, then gradually dissipated, leaving only the normal gymnasium sounds and a silence that now felt charged, stunned.

Into that silence, Max barked twice—sharp, distinct, affirmative.

Martha recovered first. "I believe," she said, her voice carrying, "your research just provided its own demonstration."

Mr. Peterson blinked rapidly. "Unusual... atmospheric refraction," he stammered, conviction absent. "Dust particles..."

"Or," Dr. Chen suggested gently, looking at Molly with pride, "perhaps some things exceed current understanding. Your methodology remains sound."

The judges moved on, visibly shaken, trying to regain composure. Mom and Dad approached, faces showing they understood precisely what occurred.

"He's making himself known more widely," Mom observed.

"Strongest right here," Dad added, gesturing to our display. "Like... endorsing your work." The thought—Sam publicly validating our attempt to understand him—felt profound.

"Did everyone see it like we did?" I wondered.

Molly's words about perception filters hung in the air. "Some saw odd light, others maybe glimpsed more."

Dad, who'd been quietly observing us. A thoughtful, almost distant look entered his eyes. He ran a hand over his chin, the way he did when puzzling over a complex blueprint. "So, it's... what you're open to, then? Or what you're meant to see?" he mused, more to himself than anyone, his voice carrying a new, reflective quality. "One person sees a flicker, another... well, another sees the whole blueprint."

The quiet weight of his words settled over me. He wasn't just accepting our experiences anymore; he was trying to understand the nature of them, the mechanics of how such things could be.

"Should get back," Mom reminded us, her voice gentle. "Martha's announcing the foundation news."

Dad turned his attention to our display board then, his eyes carefully moving over the cloud photos, then lingering on the documented anomalies. A genuine, heartfelt appreciation warmed his voice. "You two did something remarkable," he said.

"Documented something most never experience. That matters." His validation felt like a gift.

"Thanks, Dad," I managed, genuinely moved.

As Mom and Dad left, Molly retrieved her notebook. "Adding today's manifestation," she murmured. "Multiple witnesses, anomalous light/thermal properties..." Her methodical approach anchored the extraordinary.

Back at the shelter that afternoon, the transformation was tangible. Damaged sections gone, sturdy bones revealed. Signs taped to the fence: "THANK YOU EDWARD WILSON," "THE SHELTER LIVES ON." Near the entrance, a podium awaited Martha. Mayor Wilson stood nearby. The crowd was larger now.

My attention snagged on the perimeter. The single white flower now had companions—six others, spaced with mathematical precision around the property line, forming a complete circuit. Each stood in perfect bloom, defying both season and circumstance.

"The flowers," I murmured to Molly.

"Seven total," she observed, already documenting positions in her notebook. "A complete boundary."

"Like a protected space," I suggested. "Sacred ground."

Max moved with deliberate purpose from flower to flower,

examining each before positioning himself precisely in the center of the property, facing the podium. Not just present— participating.

Mom joined us. "Only three when I left," she said, gesturing toward the blooms. "They're multiplying faster."

"As renovation progresses," I noted. "His influence expanding."

Martha approached the podium. Quiet fell. Pastor John, Francis Chen, the Jenkinses, even Josh Miller were there. News had traveled.

"Friends, neighbors," Martha began, voice steady. "Many supported Maple Street through difficult times. Today, uncertainty ends." She explained the trust's discovery— framing it as foresight, fortunate timing, omitting the supernatural. Only the core group knew Sam's role, though Martha's glances toward the glowing flowers hinted otherwise. "With these funds," she continued, "we complete renovations and establish a sustainable foundation. Edward's vision—a haven where animals and humans find each other—will continue."

Applause. Martha gently raised her hands. "And a new initiative," she announced, her warm, appreciative eyes seeking out and settling on our family. "The Max Fund, fueled by your generosity, will support adoptions for families with financial need and specialized care for animals requiring it." More applause. The redirection resonated.

"Finally," Martha concluded, "the renovated shelter will include a special memorial garden dedicated to a remarkable animal whose spirit embodies everything we stand for. Sam's Garden will remind us that bonds transcend ordinary understanding and continue to guide us."

At Sam's name, the garden air stirred, though no wind blew. A sweet, unfamiliar fragrance drifted through the crowd— reminiscent of spring blooms yet distinct, comforting. Across the grounds, shadows took on unnatural precision, creating impressions of movement though nothing physical moved. One shadow commanded everyone's attention— unmistakably canine, tracing the exact path where the seven white flowers stood. Cast by no visible entity, it moved with purposeful joy before halting beside Martha.

"And it appears," she spoke into the microphone, remarkably unfazed, "our special guardian approves."

A wave of reaction rippled through the crowd—wonder, confusion, recognition. Some blinked rapidly, exchanged whispered comments with neighbors. Pastor John smiled knowingly. Francis Chen removed his glasses, wiping them slowly, his expression transforming to quiet reverence. The shadow remained visible for several heartbeats, then dissolved as conditions returned to normal. But something fundamental had changed. A collective glimpse beyond ordinary perception.

As Martha finished, Dad found me, expression reflective. "That was him?" he asked directly. "Not just light."

"Yes."

"We focused on saving the shelter," Dad mused. "Maybe

that's just part of it. Maybe this is about changing how people see things." His insight felt profound. Sam's mission expanding.

"Like ripples," Molly suggested, joining us. "Each manifestation reaches more witnesses."

Throughout the afternoon, an almost unspoken reverence permeated the crowd touring the site. Voices were hushed, hands reached out to touch the salvaged beams with a surprising tenderness, and many paused, contemplative, before those strange, perfect blooms that defied the season. They sensed the purpose here. Maple Street was becoming a threshold.

As sunset neared, our family lingered with Martha, Pastor John, and Molly. Dad produced flashlights. "Check the flowers?" Mom suggested. We moved around the perimeter, visiting each pristine, faintly glowing blossom. Dad placed small orange flags beside each.

At the final flower near the entrance, Max froze, attention locked beyond our lights. Following his gaze, my beam hit the original cornerstone, exposed by demolition. Weathered but discernible: a small carving of a dog in profile. Startlingly like Sam.

"Not possible," Dad breathed, kneeling. "1983. Sam wasn't born."

"Unless time works differently here," Pastor John suggested. "Or presence extends beyond physical life." The implication silenced us.

"Edward commissioned that," Martha said finally, voice thick. "Never explained why. Just said it felt right. That the shelter should acknowledge its true guardian."

Its true guardian. Not just our pet. A spiritual entity connected to this place across time.

As if confirming this, a peculiar illumination emanated from the seven flowers simultaneously—intensifying until each seemed crafted from pure light, forming a radiant boundary. Within it, shadows stirred—not one dog, but many silhouettes, circling with purposeful energy. Guardians patrolling. Celebrating.

"Not just Sam," Mom whispered. "All of them."

The vision held, then faded, leaving ordinary darkness. Yet, within that darkness, a new clarity had dawned for those who had seen, a sense that the world was far more layered than they had ever believed. Sanctuary where worlds intersect.

Walking back, Max pressed against my leg—Sam's comforting pressure. I met his intelligent eyes. "We understand," I told him, knowing I spoke also to the presence guiding him. "We'll help make it what it's meant to be."

Max barked twice—affirmative—then trotted toward Martha's van.

"Will they think we're crazy?" Lyn asked suddenly. "People who weren't here?"

Dad rested a hand on her shoulder. "Some might," he acknowledged. "But others recognize truth without direct experience. And some—" he glanced toward the glowing flowers "—will have their own glimpses." His words resonated: seeing beyond isn't abandoning reason, but expanding it.

"The important thing," Mom added, arm around Lyn, "is we know."

Driving home, watching stars emerge, I thought about ancient humans seeing heroes in random lights, transforming chaos into story through connection. Maybe we were doing the same. Recognizing patterns. Finding a story of enduring love.

Our house appeared. Headlights swept Sam's grave. The white flower glowed brighter, casting gentle shadows. One shadow—long, distinct, dog-shaped—stretched toward us, circled our family, then paused, focusing intently before Max. Physical and spiritual regarded each other. A silent accord seemed to settle between them, a current of shared purpose flowing from the ethereal form to the living dog. Then the shadow faded. Max remained transformed— posture straighter, eyes deeper. He led us inside with an assured, almost regal authority. Not pet, but guide.

"Goodnight, Sam," I whispered toward the oak. "Thank you." A breeze rustled leaves.

The flower pulsed once.

Inside, I paused at my window. Something had shifted within me. The quiet that once felt so deafening, so

171

impossibly loud in its emptiness, had transformed. It wasn't absence anymore, but presence—a different kind of fullness. Sam was still with us, just speaking in a new language I was finally learning to decipher.

Clouds gathered, silvered by moonlight, holding promise. Sam watched over us still, influence expanding. Not ending, but continuation. Not goodbye, but transformation. Not loss, but love evolving into forms we were only beginning to grasp.

Chapter 13:

Bridge Between Worlds

Sunlight streamed through new skylights, illuminating the gleaming kennel floor. Where cracked concrete once held stubborn stains and drainage nightmares, smooth epoxy now flowed in calming blues. The transformation was profound. Fresh air circulated, carrying the clean, crisp whisper of pine cleaner, a welcome change from the sharp antiseptic tang of the old shelter.

I ran my hand along a newly installed half-wall. Clear panels replaced the stressful chain-link, allowing visual connection without direct confrontation. Every detail felt intentional—designed to soothe, to heal.

"Impressive, isn't it?" Dad's voice, thick with pride, came from behind me. Three intense weeks had remade this place, following plans that seemed guided by more than just architectural skill.

"It feels... right," I agreed, turning. "Like it was always meant to be this way."

Dad nodded, a profound recognition of all that had transpired dawning in his eyes.

"Edward Wilson's original vision—the plans from the box—they were almost identical to those cloud blueprints we photographed." He shook his head slightly, still grappling with the synchronicity. "Like he and Sam worked together. Across time."

The idea no longer felt outlandish. The past weeks overflowed with connections defying logic—past and present, spirit and substance, species sharing purpose beyond words.

"When do the animals return?" I asked, picturing these serene spaces filled.

"Tomorrow morning. Martha wanted everything perfect." Dad checked his watch. "Speaking of, inspection team's due soon. Final approval."

We walked through the renovated corridor toward reception. Wider now, brighter, lined with photos— adoptions, volunteers, and centrally placed, the image of the cornerstone carving, Sam's profile watching over his domain.

The reception area, once cramped, now felt welcoming— warm colors, comfortable chairs, large windows overlooking the prepared earth of Sam's Garden. Martha looked up from the front desk, poised for the inspection. Beside her sat Max, the shelter's unofficial, four-legged ambassador, radiating calm capability.

"Perfect timing," Martha greeted. "Mayor Wilson just called. Committee's five minutes out."

"Ready," Dad assured her.

The shelter's physical change mirrored a deeper community

transformation. Volunteers appearing when most needed, donations arriving uncannily timed, specialists offering services pro bono. Our family's initial mission had rippled outward, drawing others into its current.

The door chimed. Mom and Lyn arrived with cookies and lemonade. "Thought the inspectors might appreciate refreshments," Mom said, taking in the transformed space.

"Truly remarkable."

"Everyone helped," Dad deflected, though he accepted Mom's quick kiss with a pleased smile.

Lyn immediately knelt to greet Max. "Good assistant manager today?" Max responded with dignified restraint, seemingly aware of his role here.

Vehicles arrived. Mayor Wilson emerged, followed by two officials with clipboards—county animal welfare and building code enforcement. Final hurdle.

"Places," Martha murmured, a hint of anxiety beneath her calm. Max positioned himself beside her, an ambassador awaiting dignitaries.

"Start here, work back," the building inspector announced, already making notes.

What followed was meticulous examination: water pressure, ventilation, drainage, exits.

Dad accompanied them, answering technical questions confidently. Martha handled operational queries. Through it all, Max remained near the kennel corridor entrance, his unwavering attention locked on the empty space beyond, radiating not anxiety, but quiet expectancy.

Waiting.

"Everything okay?" I asked, joining him.

He glanced up briefly, then refocused his intent look on the corridor. Sunlight shafting through the doorway created shifting patterns on the new floor—light and shadow moving independently, briefly suggesting spectral paw prints where nothing visible walked. Max watched, acknowledging. Sam was here. A spiritual escort for this reopening.

"He's here," I whispered. "Checking things."

Max responded with two distinct barks—low and controlled, yet perfectly clear, carrying that affirmative cadence—drawing a brief glance from the inspectors before they resumed examining ductwork. Mom drifted over, a look of quiet acknowledgment and shared knowing in her eyes.

"Felt it earlier," she confessed. "That familiar warmth." Her hand rested on my shoulder.

"He's very present today."

Nearly an hour passed. The group returned to reception. The building inspector closed her clipboard decisively. "Full compliance," she announced. "In fact, these renovations exceed current standards, particularly ventilation and sanitation."

The animal welfare inspector added her clear affirmation. "Living conditions significantly improved. Stress-reduction elements represent best practices."

Martha visibly relaxed. "Approved to welcome animals back tomorrow?"

"Absolutely." The building inspector handed over the certificate of occupancy. "Cleared for full operations."

A collective exhale filled the room. Relief. Accomplishment. The mayor offered congratulations. Max politely offered his paw.

"Maple Street has served this community for forty years," Mayor Wilson declared warmly. "Thanks to your efforts, it will continue for generations."

As the officials left, the atmosphere shifted. Tension yielded to quiet celebration. Tomorrow, the animals returned. Purpose renewed.

"We should commemorate this," Mom suggested. "Something now."

"A small gathering?" Martha mused. "Pastor John? Key volunteers?"

Plans formed quickly for an impromptu evening celebration. As they coordinated, I found myself drawn back to the kennel corridor. Ready, yes. But still feeling... incomplete. Max appeared silently beside me. Together, we walked toward kennel twenty. Sam's kennel. The discovery site. The threshold.

The space looked like the others, yet felt distinctly different. Thinner air. Charged stillness. As we approached, the atmosphere within the kennel seemed to condense, creating a pocket of heightened clarity. Within this space, particles swirled in organized patterns—too deliberate for dust—momentarily forming shapes: dogs, cats, a bird, appearing and dissolving. Max sat, watching intently, acknowledging what I only partially glimpsed.

"Remarkable, isn't it?" Martha's voice, soft behind me. She observed the phenomenon with calm acceptance.

"Sam stayed here," I noted.

A slow, thoughtful agreement settled in Martha's expression. "Six weeks," she affirmed, her voice soft with the weight of this new understanding. "Longer than usual. I often wondered why. Now I know—he was waiting for your family."

"Because we needed him?" I asked. "Or because we'd need him later, for this?"

"Perhaps both," Martha mused. "Edward believed some animals serve as guides, messengers between worlds."

As she spoke, the air pressure seemed to shift, the invisible boundary expanding to encompass us. The swirling patterns coalesced. For a stunning, suspended heartbeat, Sam materialized within the space—transparent yet vividly detailed, intelligent eyes meeting ours.

"Hello, old friend," Martha whispered. "We've done it. The shelter is renewed."

The image held, radiating benevolent presence, then slowly dissolved back into swirling light that gradually faded. Ordinary illumination returned, but the kennel felt consecrated.

"I think," Martha said into the contemplative silence, "this kennel needs a special purpose. Not regular housing. A place for animals needing extra support. Recovering from trauma."

"A healing space," I suggested, the words feeling right. "Where the boundary is thin enough for... extra help."

Her expression confirmed deep resonance. "Yes. A sanctuary."

Dad called from reception—guests arriving. We returned, leaving the kennel silent but inhabited, guardianship acknowledged.

The evening unfolded warmly. Pastor John brought cider. The Chens arrived with Molly. Volunteers shared food and stories. Max moved among guests with a calm, watchful purpose, occasionally checking the kennel corridor. A conscious participant. A bridge.

As twilight neared, Pastor John suggested, "Shall we visit the garden area?"

We moved outside. Pavers wound through prepared soil around the central white pedestal awaiting its plaque. The space felt expectant, humming.

Flowers arrive tomorrow," Martha noted. "White petunias,

lavender." No one mentioned the seven unbidden blooms already marking the perimeter, their faint, otherworldly glow now more pronounced in the fading light of dusk.

As we stood contemplating, Max alerted—head up, ears pricked, his unwavering focus instantly locking onto the garden's center. Following the line of his intently fixed stare, we watched, stunned, as a tendril of pure light emerged from the empty soil. It grew, unfurling luminous leaves, then blossoming into a flower identical to the boundary markers, but crafted entirely of light. A spiritual template. It cast a gentle, ethereal radiance, illuminating our faces.

"Well," Pastor John breathed after a moment of collective awe. "Seems the garden has already begun." No one questioned. We had moved beyond needing rational explanation. The luminous flower held, then faded, leaving only twilight and prepared earth, yet the space felt irrevocably blessed.

Our gathering dispersed slowly, carrying the warmth of shared purpose. I lingered with Max. The air felt vibrant. When he wagged his tail at empty air, I simply accepted it.

"We'll take good care of it," I promised the unseen presence. "The shelter, the garden. We understand." As if in answer, a fleeting, familiar scent brushed past—Sam's clean-dog fragrance—lingering just long enough for confirmation. Max barked twice—affirmative—then turned toward the parking lot. Mom waited in the car.

Driving home, Max dozed while Mom and I sat in comfortable silence. "Been thinking," Mom said as we turned onto our street. "How it all connects."

"Meaning?"

"The way Sam has been with us, the flowers, the renovation, Max... it feels like we're being shown something about existence. How life continues. Connections across boundaries."

"Like the shelter is becoming... a demonstration site?" I offered. "Where others might glimpse what we have?"

"Exactly," Mom affirmed. "Not everyone will see. But for those ready... glimpses across the veil." Maple Street: not just haven, but threshold.

"Tomorrow will be interesting," I observed. "Animals returning."

"Suspect some will perceive more than others," Mom replied, turning off the engine. "Just like people."

At home, Max went immediately to the oak, settling near the glowing white flower. Moonlight linked them—physical and botanical expressions of spiritual continuity.

That night, my dreams were vivid: the renovated shelter filled with animals aware of unseen presences. Kennel twenty pulsed with calm light. And Sam moved visibly among them—not ghost, but guide—helping each acknowledge its purpose in this extraordinary place.

Morning dawned warm, clear. Reopening day. Animals returning. Adoptions resuming. A milestone.

Downstairs, Dad packed a picnic basket. Lyn darted about,

gathering tournament gear.

"Morning, Will," Dad greeted. "Thought I'd drop by the shelter later. Animals arrive around ten." His casual tone belied the significance. Witnessing mattered.

"Can come too," I offered. "Last day of school."

"Perfect. Head over after dropping Lyn."

Max watched, knowing. As Lyn dashed out, he followed Dad with quiet purpose.

"Someone knows it's shelter day," Mom observed. "Meet you both there after my appointment."

By ten-fifteen, we arrived at the bustling shelter. Vans unloaded carriers. Volunteers guided animals. Martha directed traffic. Max leaped out, assuming his post beside Martha, assessing each arrival.

"Good morning!" Martha called. "Need help with the larger dogs!"

Dad and I took leashes for two goldens. Guiding them inside, I watched their reaction—excitement yielding to curious stillness as they entered the kennel corridor. Each paused, sensing something. The retrievers grew focused, ears forward, noses lifted.

"They know," Dad murmured. "Sense him." His easy acceptance still felt remarkable.

We settled the dogs. They explored, then lay down calmly.

Similar scenes unfolded—cats exploring new habitats, small animals adjusting, dogs settling quickly.

"Remarkable difference," Martha observed later. "Adjusting so fast. Like they recognize it."

"Or like it's been... consecrated," Dad suggested, the word fitting perfectly.

Martha nodded. "Edward would say the space holds presence. Animals perceive."

Throughout the morning, the pattern held: every animal paused passing kennel twenty. Not fear. Reverence.

By midday, all twenty-eight returnees were settled. Volunteers gathered for lunch, marveling. "They sense it's special," one offered. "Good energy."

"Especially kennel twenty," another added. "Every single one reacted." Knowing smiles passed among the long-timers.

Following the midday meal, Martha beckoned Dad and me toward her administrative space. Max accompanied us, positioning himself strategically beside her desk. "There's an important matter requiring discussion before the garden ceremony," she began, extracting a document folder from her drawer. "Regarding kennel twenty's designated function." She presented architectural renderings showing structural adaptations—integrated seating areas, ambient illumination systems. "After yesterday's manifestation... specialized modifications acknowledging the space's exceptional metaphysical properties. Practical for rehabilitation purposes."

Dad examined the technical drawings with professional interest. "A dedicated therapeutic environment?"

"Essentially, yes. But with additional considerations for those possessing... heightened sensitivity." Martha selected her terminology with deliberate precision. "Animals particularly receptive to the unique energetic qualities present in that space." Kennel twenty conceptualized as healing center. Interdimensional threshold. Sacred sanctuary.

"Can start modifications next week," Dad offered, already calculating.

"Wonderful, Albert. Board approved funds."

As they discussed details, my gaze drifted to Max at the window overlooking the garden space. He watched intently. Joining him, I saw flowers being unloaded—white petunias, lavender. Beyond them, shimmering outlines appeared above the soil—a translucent garden blueprint, radiant, ephemeral. Animal forms moved joyfully within it before fading.

"See that?" I whispered to Max. His subtle tail movement confirmed it.

Mom arrived then, bringing news. "Julianne Peters from Children's Services called," she announced. "Want to establish a therapy program here—children with emotional challenges interacting with animals."

Martha looked up sharply. "A formal program?"

"That's right," Mom affirmed, her expression brightening with the possibility. "Substantial grant, but they lack the facilities. Julianne heard about our renovation..."

"Remarkable timing," Martha observed, glancing at Dad and me. Synchronicity. Children needing connection. Here.

"Pilot program this summer," Mom continued. "A few children initially."

"Kennel twenty," I said at once. "The modifications—perfect."

Dad agreed. "Incorporate therapeutic considerations." Plans solidified. Shelter evolving into healing center.

Max moved to the doorway, attention fixed on the kennel corridor. A shaft of sunlight illuminated kennel twenty's entrance—a threshold of light. Within it, shadow patterns suggested movement, purpose, joy. Max watched, acknowledging.

"Will?" Mom's voice pulled me back. "Julianne mentioned a challenging case—a ten-year-old boy, Eli. Hasn't spoken since losing his father." Grief. Barriers. Need for connection beyond convention.

"I think," Martha said softly, "Eli might benefit from time in kennel twenty. Perhaps with one of our special residents." The framework emerged: kennel, therapy program, evolving mission.

As we prepared to leave, Max made a final circuit, pausing longest at kennel twenty, as if acknowledging the unique energy that now permeated that hallowed space, before rejoining us, duty done.

"He'll be back for planting," Dad told Martha.

"Wouldn't miss it," Mom added. "Another important threshold." Apt word.

That evening, beneath the oak, the white flower glowing, we shared the day's events.

"Puzzle pieces fitting," Lyn observed, muddy from her tournament. "But the puzzle's way bigger."

"That's how important things work," Dad mused. "Start small, expand. Ripples." His philosophical turn felt earned now.

Twilight deepened. The flower's radiance intensified. Shadows stirred. One drew our gaze—dog-shaped, Sam's proportions, circling us before settling beside Max. Physical, spiritual, mirroring each other. Sentinels. We acknowledged the visitation silently.

Grateful.

Tomorrow, Sam's garden. Tonight, we sat transformed, accompanied by guardians moving between worlds. The shadow faded, shifting beyond sight but remaining present. Max relaxed. Perception expanded. The way we saw the world had irrevocably shifted; a new, profound certainty about the connections all around us took firm root.

"Should get inside," Mom suggested finally. We rose, connected. The flower's glow lit our path. Clouds gathered, holding promise.

Chapter 14:

Legacy

The morning of the garden dedication arrived bathed in perfect June clarity, the sky an unblemished azure canvas stretching infinitely overhead. I woke earlier than necessary, restless with anticipation, watching dawn gradually illuminate my bedroom ceiling. The last few months felt simultaneously like moments and lifetimes— from crushing grief to those ethereal white blooms that defied all explanation, from cloud visions to shelter renovations. We'd traversed an extraordinary journey guided by an even more extraordinary navigator.

After breakfast, while Mom coaxed a reluctant Lyn into "appropriate garden dedication attire" and Dad loaded folding chairs into the truck, I slipped outside alone. The grass sparkled with dew as I crossed the yard to kneel beside Sam's grave. The white flower beneath the oak remained as pristine as the day it had impossibly emerged from the soil, its petals luminous against the morning shadows. Not a single sign of wilting or aging, defying botanical reality with each passing day.

"Big day, buddy," I murmured, running my fingers gently over the cool earth. "Your garden gets planted today. The shelter's transformed—you wouldn't recognize the place." I paused, feeling slightly self-conscious yet compelled to continue. "I keep wondering if this was your plan all along, even before... before you left us. If somehow you knew what was coming and were preparing us."

No visible response manifested, yet the quality of the morning sunlight seemed to shift subtly, taking on a warmth that transcended mere temperature, a presence perceived through senses beyond the conventional five. The breeze stilled completely, creating a pocket of perfect silence around the grave. In that moment, I understood with absolute clarity that Sam was not gone but transformed— not absent but operating from a different plane of existence. The realization settled in me not as wishful thinking but as undeniable truth.

Max materialized beside me, a shadow detaching from the deeper shade of the oak, his paws making no sound on the soft grass. He approached the white flower with a quiet reverence, nose twitching as he took a deliberate, respectful sniff. Then, as if a silent call had reached him, he pivoted.

His body tensed, ears pricked, his unwavering stare fixed eastward toward the shelter, every line of him taut with an energy that vibrated in the still morning air. Ready. The single word resonated in my own chest. Watching him, a sense of clarity settled over me, profound and peaceful.

This wasn't just about remembering Sam anymore, or even just saving a place. We were forging something new from the space he'd left behind—a pathway, perhaps, between what we knew and what lay just beyond sight.

Rising to my feet, I felt strangely lighter yet more grounded than I had in months. "Let's go," I told Max, who trotted ahead as we returned to where the family waited. Ready for the next chapter in a story that was clearly far from finished.

The shelter parking lot overflowed—not just volunteers, but townspeople drawn by the story, the sense that something significant was unfolding here. Mayor Wilson, the Chens, the Jenkinses, families from school, faces from downtown businesses—a true community gathering.

"The Thomases!" Martha called, waving us toward the garden space where tools and flats of flowers waited. "Guests of honor!" Her public framing remained careful— acknowledging our role in the practical turnaround, while the more profound, hidden truth resonated among those prepared to sense it.

The garden area hummed with potential. Prepared soil, stone pathways, the simple white pedestal awaiting its plaque. The air felt different here—charged, expectant.

"Feels consecrated already," Pastor John observed beside me. "Like the planting just confirms what's established."

Martha stepped to the modest podium. A hush of anticipation settled over the assembled crowd. "Friends, neighbors," she began, her voice clear and warm. "Thank you for joining us. Today we dedicate Sam's Garden, honoring a remarkable animal whose spirit embodies Maple Street's heart."

She spoke briefly of the garden's purpose—a place for reflection, a tribute, a symbol of renewal—carefully navigating the line between public appreciation and the private awareness of the full, miraculous truth.

"The Thomas family," she continued, "instrumental in our shelter's transformation, suggested this garden." Polite applause followed.

Martha invited Dad forward to unveil the bronze plaque on the pedestal. He approached with a quiet solemnity I hadn't often seen in him, his usual contractor's efficiency replaced by a more deliberate care. His hand, steady now where it had once trembled in the face of the inexplicable, reached for the simple cloth.

As he drew it away, his gaze lingered on the newly revealed words, and I saw his throat work, just once, before he stepped back, a subtle nod to Martha acknowledging the moment's shared significance.

SAM'S GARDEN Dedicated to all beloved companions who guide us through life's journey and remain with us in ways beyond ordinary understanding. "Love builds bridges between worlds."

"Now," Martha announced, "we invite everyone to participate in planting Sam's Garden. Each flower symbolizes the profound connection between humans and animals that brings meaning to both lives. Mr. Henderson has contributed several extraordinary specimens to complement our standard varieties."

As Martha's last word hung in the air, a hush fell, but it wasn't just the crowd quieting.

The very quality of the sunlight seemed to change, growing more golden, as if filtered through unseen layers. Then, a barely-there scent, like ozone after a distant storm mixed

191

with the sweet, unfamiliar perfume of those seven sentinel blooms, drifted through the onlookers.

Necks prickled.

A few people glanced upward at the cloudless sky, a slight frown of puzzlement touching their lips. Then, the warmth settled in—not just the sun, but a gentle, enveloping heat that wrapped the gathering in a comforting embrace. At the same instant, a collective intake of breath could be heard as, one by one, heads turned towards the shelter's perimeter.

The seven white flowers there had begun to tremble, their petals vibrating with an inner light, and a low, melodic hum emerged, less a sound heard with the ears and more a thrum felt deep in the chest, resonating up from the ground itself. That's when the murmurs began, a wave of hushed whispers rippling through the stunned assembly.

"What are those flowers?" someone asked aloud. "Are they... glowing?"

Before Martha could answer, old Mr. Henderson, the nursery owner, stepped forward, his weathered face calm. "Those," he announced, his voice carrying easily, "are why I brought these."

From his truck, he retrieved a tray holding seven small plants, unlike any nursery stock I'd ever seen. Each bore a single, tightly closed bud that seemed to vibrate faintly; the stems shone with an unusual silver-white luster.

"Been nurturing these forty years," Henderson continued

matter-of-factly. "Grew from seeds that just... appeared one morning in my greenhouse. Never bloomed, never propagated. Just these single buds, waiting. Knew when Martha called about this garden—these belong here." His unembellished telling of a forty-year botanical mystery that defied all known precedent silenced skepticism.

"Plant these at the center," he instructed. "A circle around the pedestal. Seven points, matching the boundary markers."

The planting proceeded with unusual harmony. People found roles naturally—children placing smaller blooms, families working together. Shared purpose transcended ordinary volunteering. Our family joined Martha, Pastor John, and Mr. Henderson at the center with the seven mysterious plants. The buds pulsed rhythmically now, the silvery stems warm to the touch. As we carefully placed the final plant, Max—who had been patrolling the garden's edge with focused intensity—stopped, alert.

A collective gasp swept the crowd. From the seven boundary flowers, luminous particles—not seeds, but points of pure light—drifted upward in spirals, scattering gently across the shelter grounds like a blessing. At the same instant, the seven newly planted buds at the garden's center began to unfurl in perfect synchrony. Petals identical to the boundary flowers opened, revealing hearts of brilliant gold that blazed in the strange light.

"Well," Henderson grunted with satisfaction. "Took 'em long enough to find their spot."

His practical tone grounded the miracle. People reacted

variously—open astonishment, quiet tears, knowing glances, bewildered shrugs.

"The newly opened blossoms stabilized, their initial brilliance gently subsiding to a steady, pearlescent luminescence, clearly permanent features now. The golden light bathing the garden gradually yielded to normal sunshine.

"As you can see," Martha announced, voice admirably steady, "Sam's Garden will be... quite special. A place for connection, for remembering."

During the reception that followed, amidst lemonade and cookies, Martha shared more.

The Max Fund," Martha explained, her voice warm, "established with your generous donations, will help families for whom a special animal connection might make all the difference."

Her hand swept toward kennel twenty. Just then, a staff member emerged, gently leading a young dog into the afternoon light. My breath hitched. It was the way he moved, a certain confident yet gentle inquiry in his stance. Predominantly white, one ear flopped with the exact same charming lack of symmetry Sam had possessed, and his eyes... they held that same soulful, knowing light, mirroring the keen, intelligent awareness I remembered so vividly from our own puppy.

Beside me, I sensed rather than saw Mom and Dad exchange a startled glance; a silent question and a dawning, shared recognition of the impossible familiarity passed between them, the same one now thundering in my own chest.

"This special resident arrived last week," Martha continued. "Found wandering near the highway, he immediately showed unusual calm and settled right into kennel twenty." The white dog surveyed the gathering with a composed awareness that seemed beyond his years. His gaze eventually settled on a quiet family standing near the edge of the crowd—a mother and three children, the youngest a boy of about ten who stood slightly apart, eyes fixed on the ground.

What happened next unfolded with such natural grace that it felt choreographed. The white dog, still on his leash, gently led the handler directly to the boy. The crowd parted instinctively. When they reached the child, the dog sat down and waited, his focus unwavering.

The boy—who hadn't looked up during the entire ceremony—slowly raised his eyes. Something passed between child and dog, a silent communication almost palpable to those watching. Then, with deliberate care, the dog lifted his paw, placing it on the boy's hand.

The mother's soft gasp was audible in the hush that had fallen. She knelt beside her son, one hand covering her mouth, eyes bright with emotion.

"Eli," she whispered, "do you want to say hello?"

The boy studied the dog for a long moment. His hand turned, accepting the paw in a gentle handshake. Then something remarkable happened—his expression shifted, subtly at first, like ice beginning to thaw. His lips moved, forming words that at first made no sound.

The dog leaned forward slightly, as if listening. Encouraged by this attention, the boy tried again.

"Bridge," he said, the single word clear though barely above a whisper.

His mother's eyes filled with tears. One of his sisters stepped closer, placing a supportive hand on his shoulder.

"What did you say, sweetheart?" his mother asked, her voice gentle with wonder.

The boy kept his gaze on the dog, who hadn't moved, hadn't broken their bond.

"His name is Bridge," he said, each word careful but certain. "He... helps me."

Later, as the crowd dispersed into smaller conversations, Martha approached our family privately. "That was Eli's first spoken word in almost a year," she confided. "His mother Jane told me they lost his father suddenly last year. Eli was there when it happened." Martha's voice held deep respect for the family's privacy. "She's been bringing him to therapists, but nothing reached him until Bridge."

The white dog—now officially named Bridge—remained beside Eli throughout the afternoon. I watched them from a distance, noting how the boy's posture had changed. Still soft-spoken when he chose to speak, still careful in his movements, but somehow more present, more engaged with the world around him.

As afternoon waned to evening, I noticed Eli and Bridge had moved to a quiet corner of the garden. The boy was speaking softly to the dog, his words too low for anyone to hear. Bridge listened with complete attention, occasionally placing his paw on Eli's knee when the boy fell silent.

As sunset approached and the crowd thinned, something extraordinary unfolded. Eli, previously absorbed in an almost telepathic communication with Bridge, suddenly snapped his head up, his eyes fixing intently on a point hovering just above the dog's head. His expression underwent a complete metamorphosis—astonishment, recognition, and a surge of pure, unfiltered joy that constricted my throat with emotion.

"Dad?" he whispered, fingers extending toward something imperceptible to everyone else.

Bridge pressed his body protectively against the boy, offering silent reassurance as Eli experienced something profoundly intimate. The seven central garden flowers seemed to respond, their petals quivering slightly, creating what felt like a sacred boundary encircling child and dog. Whatever connection Eli was experiencing remained entirely personal, beyond shared observation.

When his mother approached with gentle caution, Eli turned toward her, his eyes containing both welling tears and— remarkably—the first genuine smile I'd witnessed from him.

"Bridge helps me connect with Dad," he explained with childlike simplicity. "Not absent. Just... existing differently."

I glanced at my own mother. Tears were silently tracing paths down her cheeks, but her expression was one of profound, almost radiant empathy. She reached out, not to Eli, but to Dad, her hand finding his and gripping it tightly, a shared, unspoken acknowledgment of the miracle unfolding before them and the echoes of their own journey.

The main gathering began to break apart, the collective sound of voices fraying at the edges before dissolving into the murmur of smaller conversations. My gaze drifted, finding Eli and Bridge near the new sapling at the garden's edge.

The boy stood differently now. Where before his shoulders had curved inward, a protective shell, they now seemed to rest more squarely, his chin lifted just enough to meet the world. Even the way his hand rested on Bridge's fur seemed less like clinging and more like a companionable, unspoken partnership. He was still a boy marked by sorrow, but a fragile new awareness flickered in his stance, a hesitant step back into the flow of the living.

Mom joined me, following my eyes. "Remarkable," she murmured. "One meeting with the right dog."

"Not just any dog," I reminded her. "A bridge."

A week later, when Eli and his mother Jane returned for their first official visit, Martha invited our family to observe from the office. The boy who entered was noticeably different from the silent child at the garden dedication. Though still quiet, his eyes now engaged with his surroundings, his hand steady on Bridge's lead.

"He's started speaking more at home," Jane confided to Mom while Eli and Bridge settled in kennel twenty—the space now temporarily designated for their sessions. "Not just about Bridge. About his father too. Memories he's kept locked inside for months."

Through the observation window, we watched as Eli sat cross-legged on the floor, Bridge attentive beside him. The boy's lips moved in conversation too quiet to hear.

"What's he doing?" Dad asked softly.

"Telling Bridge about his dad," Jane explained, eyes bright with restrained emotion. "He says Bridge can see him, can... deliver messages." She hesitated. "I know it sounds—"

"It doesn't sound strange at all," Mom assured her, placing a gentle hand on the woman's shoulder. "Not to us."

As we watched, something extraordinary unfolded. The quality of light in kennel twenty seemed to shift, creating a gentle radiance around the boy and dog. Bridge suddenly sat alert, ears pricked, his unwavering attention zeroed in on the empty air beside Eli.

The boy's expression transformed—recognition, joy, and a profound peace washing over his features. His hand reached out, touching a space where nothing was visible to us.

"Dad's here," Jane whispered, not surprised but awed. "Eli says he can always feel him with Bridge nearby, but sometimes... sometimes he can actually see him."

Martha joined us at the window. "Eli's not the only one," she said. "Since the renovation, we've had three other children report similar experiences in that space. Each time with specially selected dogs. It's becoming something of a pattern."

"The thin place is growing thinner," Dad observed, his acceptance of the inexplicable now complete. "Sam's doing?"

"Sam's legacy," Martha corrected gently. "A door once opened doesn't easily close."

Over the following months, Eli's progress accelerated. By summer, he had returned to school, joined a children's grief support group where he spoke openly about Bridge's special abilities, and even helped Martha design a brochure for what was becoming known as the "Companion Connection Program."

The success didn't go unnoticed. Children's Services referred more cases; the waiting list grew. What had begun as one boy finding his voice through a special dog was evolving into something neither Martha nor we could have anticipated—a structured program where children experiencing traumatic loss connected with carefully selected animals who seemed uniquely attuned to the space between worlds.

Martha formally announced that the Max Fund would cover Bridge's adoption and ongoing care. As she spoke, I realized we were witnessing exactly what Sam had been guiding us toward—not just saving a building, but creating a space where healing connections could form, where bridges between worlds might be built.

The simple, profound statement hung in the silence. Bridge placed his paw again on Eli's hand. Deliberate comfort. Connection.

"Yes," Martha agreed gently, meeting the boy's gaze with complete understanding. "Some special animals help us see beyond ordinary eyes."

Around Eli and Bridge, a subtle radiance gathered. Within it, a shadow formed—larger than Bridge, familiar stance, unmistakably Sam—present for moments before dissolving. Max, sitting nearby, acknowledged the visitation with two quiet tail thumps. Mom gasped. Dad's hand rested on my shoulder, a silent confirmation.

"Sam," I whispered.

"Connecting them," Mom breathed back. "Building the bridge." The name—Eli's name for the dog—resonated with sudden, deep significance.

Later, as the crowd thinned and evening approached, our family lingered in the garden with Martha and Pastor John. The seven central flowers glowed, defining sacred space.

"I think I see better now," I said into the comfortable silence. "Why Sam stayed connected. It wasn't just us, or saving the shelter."

"No," Pastor John agreed. "Though those were part of his mission."

"He's creating... infrastructure," I ventured, the concept clarifying as I spoke. "Bridges between worlds. The garden, kennel twenty, the flowers—access points."

Martha nodded. "Edward used to call certain souls 'architects between realms'—creating pathways others follow."

"Like Bridge and Eli," Mom observed. "That dog is literally helping Eli connect."

Above the pedestal, light gathered—not from any external source but self-generating, coalescing with an internal hum that seemed to vibrate in the very air around us. All other sound—the evening breeze, distant traffic, even our own breathing—seemed to fall away into an absolute, reverent stillness.

Within that charged silence, Sam appeared. Not shadow, not suggestion, but a being of palpable, luminous substance. Translucent, yes, but undeniably there, defined in every detail from the soft wave in his white fur to the distinctive flop of one ear, to the profound, intelligent awareness evident in his gaze.

This manifestation felt different—deliberate, intended for all of us. An almost palpable wave of pure, unconditional love flowed outward from him, settling over our small group like a gentle embrace, bringing tears to my eyes.

Beside me, Mom's breath hitched into a soft, choked sob. Her shoulders trembled, and one hand rose, palm open and fingers slightly outstretched—not to touch the ethereal form, but as if to feel the very air he displaced, to affirm the beautiful, heartbreaking reality of his presence. Tears streamed unchecked down her face, yet her expression, when she briefly met my eyes, was one of utter, radiant peace.

For perhaps thirty seconds, he stood fully manifest, his attention moving between us—Mom, Dad, Lyn, Martha, Pastor John, me—a conscious, loving connection. Then, his focus shifted entirely to Max. Silent communication passed between them, the air between them seeming to vibrate with meaning. Max's posture straightened, ears forward, his entire being suffused with a solemn acceptance, a profound readiness. A passing of the torch. A blessing.

His duty acknowledged, Sam turned toward the shelter entrance where Eli and his family prepared to leave with Bridge. Though distant, his attention was unmistakably fixed. The air around him seemed to ripple, then a path of disturbed grass formed—as if traced by invisible paws—stretching across the grounds, reaching the boy and his new guardian before settling.

With an air of utter peace and satisfied resolution, Sam's form began to change—not vanishing, but transitioning, becoming a fine mist that spiraled outward, merging with the soil, the flowers, the very air of the garden, seeding the space with his enduring essence. The subtle vibration we'd all felt faded, leaving behind a silence that felt richer, more resonant than before.

"Well," Dad said finally, breaking the profound silence, "guess that settles any lingering questions about imagining things." His dry remark cut the tension. Gentle laughter rippled through our small group.

"That felt... foundational," Martha observed reflectively. "Establishing something permanent."

"Consecrating the space," Pastor John agreed.

As darkness settled, the seven central flowers intensified their glow, illuminating the garden. "Sam's Garden will be more than a memorial," Martha stated. "A place where people find what they need."

"A thin place," Pastor John suggested. "Where heaven and earth touch."

"A bridge," Mom added softly.

"Exactly what Sam intended," I concluded, watching Max return to the garden's center, taking up position beside the pedestal. Guardian on duty. "Creating spaces where others can experience connection. Where love passes through."

As we finally prepared to leave, clouds gathered on the horizon, silvered by the rising moon, promising tomorrow's patterns. "Thank you," I whispered toward the garden, the shelter, the sky, the presence beyond sight. "For everything."

Walking to our cars, Max trotted ahead purposefully, glancing back to ensure we followed. Not replacement, but continuation. Not ending, but evolution.

As our car pulled away, I looked back one final time. The garden had transformed in the gathering dusk—the seven blossoms now standing like silent sentinels at a threshold between worlds. They seemed to pulse with each passing breeze, as though breathing in harmony. And somewhere in that sacred space between seen and unseen, I sensed Sam's spirit still vibrantly alive within it—no longer just watching, but woven into the very essence of this place, his energy echoing in every connection formed here.

The road curved, and the shelter disappeared from view, but the certainty remained: what Sam had created here would endure, just as love itself endures. Not an ending, but a continuation; not absence, but transformation. I hoped with all my heart that everyone, somewhere, had a Sam in their life—a love that guides, protects, and remains even when everything else changes. A love that builds bridges between worlds and reminds us that goodbye is never the final word.

Epilogue:

Full Circle

The university campus lay still and settled under a late spring sky as the conference reception wound down. Stars pricked the deepening velvet overhead—a canvas I'd scanned for patterns since boyhood, though these days more out of habit than necessity. The air carried the scent of new possibilities after days spent discussing research that traced its origins back to those cloud formations that once so clearly defied all meteorology and a white dog named Sam.

A soft, familiar nudge against my leg. "Hey, Bridge," I murmured, scratching behind the ears of the sturdy Lab mix at my side. Not the original Bridge, of course—Eli Jensen's childhood companion had passed years ago. Yet the tradition continued unbroken; there had always been a Bridge at Maple Street Center, each carrying that name and the remarkable intuitive awareness that connected so intrinsically with our work. Tonight's companion—Bridge III—leaned against me with reassuring solidarity.

I adjusted my conference badge: Dr. William Thomas, Keynote Speaker. The title still felt borrowed, though my research on interspecies connection and grief recovery had gained unexpected recognition in both scientific and spiritual communities.

"Dr. Thomas?"

I turned to find a young woman, perhaps twenty, clutching a worn copy of my book. The cover showed a simple white flower against a cloud-scattered sky.

"I'm sorry to bother you," she began, her voice unsteady. "I just... your book saved me last year. After my cat died."

I gestured to the empty chair beside me. "Not a bother at all. Tell me about your cat."

"Marmalade," she said, sitting down. "Seventeen years. I got him when I was five."

"A lifetime companion," I acknowledged. "The hardest to lose."

Her chin dipped in a small, almost painful affirmation, fingers tracing the book's edge.

"Everyone told me, 'It was just a cat.' But your book understood. And then..." She hesitated, glancing around as if fearing judgment. "Two weeks after, I found a perfect orange feather on my pillow. No birds in the house, windows closed. It smelled like him."

"And you knew," I finished.

"Yes." Relief flooded her face. "I knew he was still... somewhere. Somehow." She pressed the book toward me. "Would you sign it? To Jessie?"

As I signed, Bridge shifted position, his attention fixing on a point just beyond the young woman's shoulder. His ears pricked forward, head tilting in that familiar way that still made my heart catch. Following his gaze, I saw nothing visible—but I'd learned decades ago that "visible" had limited meaning.

"He sees something, doesn't he?" Jessie whispered, following my eyes.

"Bridge has excellent perception," I replied carefully, returning her book. "Sometimes better than mine."

"Can I..." She reached tentatively toward Bridge, who immediately transferred his attention to her, pressing his head against her outstretched hand. The contact brought tears to her eyes.

"Thank you," she managed. "For everything."

After she left, Bridge and I made our way across campus to the modest apartment the university provided visiting lecturers. Tomorrow I'd return home to the renovated farmhouse near Maple Street Center, where Mom and Dad—both in their seventies but still remarkably vital—continued to be involved with the shelter's operations.

Dad had semi-retired from his construction company five years ago, though his practical skills were still sought for special projects—particularly animal care facilities. He'd arrive on site, blueprints in hand, and I'd hear him, his voice carrying the same no-nonsense tone he once used for load-bearing walls, now earnestly explaining to younger architects how specific orientations of light and space could create what he termed 'threshold principles'—areas conducive to a... quieter kind of connection. His journey from hard-headed skeptic to this earnest advocate remained one of the most profound transformations I'd witnessed.

I'd often find him on-site at the newer Maple Street Center expansions, or even at other facilities that had sought his unique consultation, patiently pointing out to a group of initially bewildered contractors how the angle of a window wasn't just about morning light, but about creating a 'thin space,' or how a particular water feature could 'soothe the veil,' as he'd taken to calling it. He'd tap the blueprints with a calloused finger, his arguments grounded as much in observed animal behavior at our Center as in any mystical theory.

In my apartment, Bridge settled on the rug while I opened my laptop. The manuscript of my new book glowed on the screen, tentatively titled "Beyond the Veil: Understanding Continued Bonds After Loss." Twenty-five years of collected stories from the Center—children finding healing through animal bonds, elderly residents describing visits from departed pets, documented cases of animals perceiving what humans couldn't.

What had begun as a grieving boy's journal had evolved into a life's work. The Center now hosted researchers from around the world studying the unique properties of what we'd learned to call "threshold spaces"—areas where the membrane between worlds grew thin. Kennel twenty remained the most active site, though the garden and several other locations demonstrated similar qualities.

Lyn's international soccer camps for underprivileged youth now incorporated animal therapy components. Mom's careful documentation had created protocols used globally.

Even Pastor John, well into his eighties, still conducted monthly services in the garden chapel.

And Sam? His presence had evolved over the decades—less dramatic manifestation, more steady undercurrent. The white flowers continued to bloom year-round, impervious to seasons. Occasionally, on significant days, cloud formations still appeared. But the constant stream of stories from those who visited the Center—glimpses, scents, dreams, feelings—suggested something far beyond a single dog's spirit. Rather, Sam had become a doorway, an opening through which countless connections now flowed in both directions.

Bridge rose suddenly, moving to the window. Outside, clouds gathered against the night sky, silvered by moonlight. Within them, shapes began to form—not random, but deliberate. Not one dog, but many. A pack running joyfully through the heavens.
"I see them too," I told him.

My phone vibrated with an incoming text from Lyn: *Pics or it didn't happen! So proud, dork. Kick science butt! PS – Donation sent. :)*

Another notification: a photo from Mom and Dad. Their smiling faces beside Martha's niece at the Center, Pastor John nearby. *Caption: We're here and ready. Dad says don't forget to mention his drainage system design in your talk.*

That made me laugh out loud—some things never changed. Dad's pride in the technical aspects of what we'd built remained as strong as ever, grounding our more esoteric work in practical reality. The perfect balance.

Gratitude washed over me—for the journey, the learning, the chance to share it. For the grieving boy I'd been and the man that grief had shaped me into becoming. For the family that had navigated this extraordinary path together, evolving but unbroken. For the dog who'd shown us that goodbye was never the final word.

The clouds shifted, forming one last shape before dispersing—an open book, pages turning in an unfelt wind. I smiled, acknowledging the message.

"C'mon, Bridge," I said softly, opening the door to the cool night air. "Let's take a walk. They're waiting."

And I knew, with a certainty born not of logic but of lived experience, that some stories never truly end—they simply continue beyond the last page, invisible except to those with hearts open enough to perceive them.

AUTHOR'S NOTE

The seed for Sam in the Clouds was intensely personal, nurtured by memories of a beloved childhood companion. As William's fictional journey unfolded, I also found myself drawing inspiration from the rich tradition of stories that explore childhood wonder, faith, and the magical connections that can lie just beyond our everyday sight.

In particular, the works of C.S. Lewis, and his Narnia chronicles, have always held a special place in my heart. His vision of faith, hope, and love transcending ordinary boundaries, and the idea that profound truths can appear in forms often dismissed as fantasy, resonated deeply as I wrote about Sam's enduring presence. If you sensed familiar literary echoes in Sam's guiding, protecting, and teaching role, or in the broader themes of the novel, you might have recognized this gentle nod to an author whose tales have captivated generations.

Thank you for joining William and his family on their journey. My hope is that Sam in the Clouds offers a sense of comfort and the possibility that love, once given, truly does transform and remain with us always.

Cameron De Jong

PS - I couldn't publish this without a photo of Sam and Mom, both who are in Heaven. These photos bring tears every time I look at them. Tears of love, joy, and peace. I love you both.

ABOUT THE AUTHOR

A successful leader in sales and marketing since 2006, with a BA in Political Science from Elon University (2002), Cameron De Jong has always understood the power of connection. Born in Bath, NY (1979) and raised in North Carolina, his journey into creative writing began in high school, driven by a desire to explore the deeper bonds that shape our lives.

This exploration is at the heart of the story you are reading. Inspired by the enduring impact of his own beloved childhood dog, it delves into the transformative power of love and the possibility of connections that reach beyond the ordinary.

When he's not leading teams or crafting narratives, Cameron enjoys traveling, basketball, and the pursuit of new knowledge. He lives in Babcock Ranch, Florida, with his partner and their three adored dogs.

Stay in touch at https://samintheclouds.com